D0944289

SOMETHING LIKE HOME

ALSO BY ANDREA BEATRIZ ARANGO

Iveliz Explains It All

SOMETHING LIKE HOME

ANDREA BEATRIZ ARANGO

RANDOM HOUSE 🏠 NEW YORK

Text copyright © 2023 by Andrea Beatriz Arango
Jacket art copyright © 2023 by Oriol Vidal

All rights reserved. Published in the United States by Random House Children's Books, a division of Penguin Random House LLC, New York.

Random House and the colophon are registered trademarks of Penguin Random House LLC.

Visit us on the Web! rhcbooks.com

Educators and librarians, for a variety of teaching tools, visit us at RHTeachersLibrarians.com

Library of Congress Cataloging-in-Publication Data is available upon request.
ISBN 978-0-593-56618-3 (trade) — ISBN 978-0-593-56619-0 (lib. bdg.) — ISBN 978-0-593-56620-6 (ebook)

Printed in the United States of America
10 9 8 7 6 5 4 3 2 1
First Edition

PARA MI MAMI—
THIS BOOK WAS BORN FROM YOUR IDEA.
TE AMO.

TIME AND SPACE

The drive to Titi's house takes exactly eighteen minutes.
I know because my current Rubik's Cube solving time
is about two minutes,
and I solve my scratched-up, faded cube
a grand total of nine times.

I can feel Janet watching me in the rearview mirror,
probably wondering if I'm okay,
and I wish for the hundredth time that I could
twist my way out of her too-clean car,
line my life back up as easily as the sides of my cube,
erase all the ways I messed up this weekend,

so that instead of driving to the rich side of town,
I'd be at my parents' bright red food truck,
and instead of a black bag of packed clothes at my feet,
I'd be dishing up plates of yellow rice for my friends.

Janet doesn't actually care how I feel.
She's just here 'cause it's her job.
So even though she offers to carry my bag
after we park,
even though I'm sweating through my shirt
and my glasses keep slipping off,

I carefully put the cube in my sweatpants pocket,
lift my bagged-up things with my own two hands,
take a deep breath, ignoring Janet,
and start walking by myself toward my aunt's door

and my weird
                    weird
                              new life.

DID YOU KNOW?

Most birds don't recognize their family members
after more than a year has passed.
So it makes sense that I'm wearing
my favorite owl shirt
as I stare at a woman I don't recognize,
but that Janet assures me is my aunt.

Titi Silvia is a doctor,
but one that looks like a model,
like the doctors on those TV shows
my mom won't ever let me watch.

And even though I usually try not to care
about the clothes I wear or how they fit,
I definitely care *today*
as I feel her staring first at my hair
and then at my wrinkled clothes,
moving down to my socks and slides
and then back up to my stomach,
like everything about me
is out of place, different
from what she'd like.

I don't know how I'm supposed to greet her,
this woman that is basically a stranger
and who looks nothing like me,

so I just shrug at her awkward hola,
wait for her to tell me where to put my stuff,
and then I leave her and Janet talking
and hide in the office,

aka my (*temporary*) new room.

MY ROOM THAT IS NOT MY ROOM

Titi Silvia's apartment is beautiful,
but it almost doesn't look real.

It's all white and clean
and full of art that makes no sense,
and I can tell my aunt's really tried to turn her office
into a bedroom for a kid,
because there's a big inflatable mattress in the middle
and she's added a princess blanket that is
pretty babyish
and way too pink,
which she probably bought
because she doesn't know what sixth graders
actually like to watch on TV.

And if I was here for different reasons,
I'd probably just laugh at the blanket
and bounce on the inflatable bed,

but the problem is,
I'm supposed to actually *live* here.

Titi Silvia already mentioned
something about Ikea and furniture
as I slid past her in the hall,

and who wants a temporary place
to act like a forever one?

Especially when that place
is with a rich perfect stranger
who the social services people keep telling you
over and over and over

      is "safer" than your parents
      is a "good" solution
      is someone you're "extremely lucky"

to have offered you a home.

MY AUNT THAT IS NOT MY AUNT

I hear Janet leave
and I pick up my cube again.
Not because I want to practice,
but more 'cause I want to have an excuse
not to talk
if Titi Silvia decides to come in.

I don't care what Janet says.
This is not where I want to be.
Especially when my aunt *does* walk in
(she doesn't even knock!)
and starts talking to me in soft Spanish
      like we're not strangers and
this is our shared language,
      like she's always been around and
this is a super-normal visit
      and not what it actually is.

All I've ever heard about my titi
is that she'd never lend Mom money
      when we needed it,
never help Mom out
      when she was sick,

and Dad always tells me
to ask when I don't know something,
to not keep my questions inside,

but even though I want to ask Titi *why,*

    why didn't you help when we needed you?
    why did you wait until now to show up in my life?

it's hard to ask questions
when you don't want to know the answers anyway,
hard to talk when your head feels like
        it's inside a bubble
and your body feels like
        shooting up into the air,

harder, even, than listening to my aunt's constant

        hola Laura, hola mi amor

and so without looking up from my Rubik's Cube,
I just lie and say:

        no hablo español.

YO SÉ

The truth is,
I do speak Spanish. A little bit.
Just not the way Titi Silvia does.

Dad was born here
and understands it better than he speaks it,
so I only ever spoke it with Mom.

And if I'm being honest,
whatever we were saying
was more of a mixed Spanglish
than whatever it is that Titi talks.

The food we sold at the food truck?
I got you.
Prices and customer service?
Nobody's ever complained.

But Titi is fast-Spanishing awkward stuff
about her recycling system
and what my new school will be like,
and it's not that I don't understand her.
I do.
But not as perfectly as I did Mom.

UNPACKING

Titi Silvia leaves me by myself to unpack,
but it's not like I brought a bunch of stuff.

How do you prepare for the unpreparable?
How do you fit your whole life in one bag?

And how am I supposed to trust social services,
trust *Janet*,
when she won't trust me back?

QUESTIONS I'VE ASKED JANET

How long will I be with my aunt?
What will happen to our trailer?
What will happen to the things I don't pack?
When can I talk to Mom?
When can I talk to Dad?
What does kinship care mean?
Why do I have a caseworker?
What even is a caseworker?
Do my parents know where I'm going?
Who knows where I'm going?
How long will I be with my aunt?

Is this because I called 911?

Is this my fault?

ANSWERS JANET HAS GIVEN ME

DID YOU KNOW?

Some birds hold funerals
for the birds in their families
that have passed away.

Other birds will cry by empty nests
for a long time
hoping that the bird that died will
     wake up
     come back
so they can all go on
with their normal bird lives.

I'm not a bird,
but in case you can't tell yet,
I kinda wish I was.
Their lives seem so much simpler
so much easier to understand.

My two-bedroom trailer is empty of people now,
     abandoned,
and all because of me.

And it feels like everyone just wants me
to move on
to be cool.

But every time I think about
me living with my aunt,
think about my Crenwood neighbors
gossiping about where we are,

all I want to do is yell
really really loud,
shout at the world that *this is not permanent*
this is not forever

this was a mistake
and my parents are getting better

and if everyone would just wait a few days
would close their eyes and go to sleep
then everything would swirl back
(like it never even happened)
and we could all pretend

nothing ever, ever changed.

RIVERVIEW ELEMENTARY SCHOOL

RES is bigger than my old school,
    nicer
    cleaner
with student artwork on every wall.

My homeroom teacher is Ms. Holm,
whose classroom is full of books and plants,
and I'm happy to realize I'll get to stay with her all day,
and not have to swap classrooms
and memorize schedules
that I know will just get me turned around.

Before? Stuff like that didn't make me nervous.
Now? I feel so lost I could almost cry.

Too many changes,
too many new things,
too many goodbyes and hellos and
silences in the dark,

and so even though I know
I'll only be at this school
for a tiny amount of time,
knowing where I'll spend my day
knowing I have one assigned desk
with my name duct-taped on,

it's not something I needed before,
but today?

It makes me feel like a little
snuggled-up parakeet.

It makes me feel calm.

PICTURE THIS

You've been in the same town
with the same kids
all the way from kindergarten
to sixth grade.

And sure,
maybe there's been a new kid here and there,
but probably not a lot
and usually at the beginning of the year.

Then imagine you get to Riverview
on a windy October day,
on your very first year of middle school,
on Picture Day (!)
when you're not expecting any more change,

and all of a sudden there's a new girl
standing in front of your class,
a girl you've never seen before
but that clearly doesn't belong here:

the food truck girl,
the fidgety girl,
the trailer girl

from all the way across town.

JUST A REGULAR, NORMAL KID

I try not to stand out,
really, I do.
I didn't know it was Picture Day
when I got dressed this morning,
but I think my plain blue jeans
and black hoodie
are okay,

the gel I used this morning
keeping my thick and wavy brown hair
in a frizzy ponytail
that is at least
semi-contained.

But I'm still the new kid,
which means Ms. Holm
asks me to introduce myself,
asks me to stand in front of the whole class,

'cause teachers somehow
still haven't figured out
how obviously terrifying
having twenty-five pairs of eyes on you is.

How it leaves you with absolutely nowhere to hide.

THE INTRODUCTION I DON'T MAKE

Hi.

My name is Laura [LAH-OO-RAH]
and I used to live on the other side
of Loumack County, Virginia,
in the Crenwood Trailer Park,
but now (and *just* for now)
I live with my aunt in this part of town.

My parents are in rehab,
which is why I'm here,
in a school that hands out
organic blueberry muffins for breakfast
and has no writing on the bathroom stalls,

in a classroom where
probably everyone has a perfect family
and nobody has any secrets

and even though I wish
you were all nice and friendly,
I have a feeling

you're not.

THE INTRODUCTION I DO MAKE

Hi,
I'm Laura [LAW-RAH].

I MISS MY FRIENDS BACK HOME

I spend my lunch period in the library,
because my amazing introduction
didn't really win me any new friends,
and as I play alone
with the basket of fidget toys
set out on one of the tables,
I wish

(for the hundredth time)

that I knew how to explain to
Remedios, Pilar, and Betsaida
that I didn't ghost them,
I got taken,
that nobody asked me or cared
what I thought about the whole thing at all,

and if it had been up to me
and not social services,
I would have stayed with my parents,

I would have never left home.

DECISIONS

I know I messed up back in Crenwood.
Janet and Titi don't have to say it out loud
for me to understand that it's true.

But just because I let my parents down
      this time
doesn't mean I will again.

And if Janet thinks I'm just going to
forget everything that happened
     she's wrong
because I already repacked
everything I had unpacked,
my black bag sitting in the closet
all ready to go.

I just have to find a way to fix this,
find a way to undo this,
and then I'll be back with Mom and Dad

and they'll be perfectly okay

and I'll never
never ever
have to make another decision
ever again.

SOMEONE IS ALWAYS WATCHING

I may not have a phone,
but I do have a laptop now,
since every student at Riverview
gets their own to take home.

And when I google Harmonic Way
(the place Janet said my parents are at),
I see pictures of smiling people
and gardens full of singing cardinals
and board games and crafts and baking,
though the Google reviews
are only at 2.9 out of 5.

I'm about to click into some of them,
the reviews,
to try to read what people have to say,
but then my neck hairs start tingling
and my arm hairs start prickling
and when I look up,
there's a kid with braids next to me at the table
smiling
and I slam my laptop shut.

TRUST IS OVERRATED

The kid introduces himself as Benson, he/him.
Says he's in sixth grade (but not my class),
and although I eye him suspiciously,
I tell him I'm Laura, she/her,
and in Ms. Holm's class.

Benson is Black and short and skinny,
but what I most notice
is his humongous smile—
like we've been friends our entire lives
and are just meeting for lunch to catch up.

And even though I'm pretty sure I'm frowning,
he still tosses his stickered water bottle
            up and down,
smiling at me in between sips,
his eyes twinkling into a laugh.

He's weird, this Benson.
Too friendly. Too nice.
But just as I'm about to make an excuse,
say something like how I need to head back to class,
the bell rings
                    (thank you, thank you)
and I hurry out,
laptop and backpack in hand.

Dad would tell me I'm being rude,
but it's not like he's here to see this anyway.
And I'm not sure what Janet from social services
would say,
but she definitely made it clear
back at my trailer
that she thought I should feel grateful
for my aunt and my new school,
which she talks about like it's
        a *forever* thing,
a "positive" change.

Basically, adults know nothing.
Nothing nothing period.

And as for me? I'm definitely not ready
to explain to anyone
and especially not any of the kids
at this rich, temporary school

why I live where I live.

MY AFTER-SCHOOL ROUTINE BECAUSE
I LIVE WITH A VERY CONTROLLING AUNT

Get off the bus at the Stonecreek Apartments
and walk to building 1380,
then climb the stairs to apartment C.

Connect my laptop to the Wi-Fi
and then message Titi at work to tell her
  I'm here
even though she could definitely
just check her doorbell camera,
which

(like I'm some sort of prisoner)

already records me on the way in.

TITI SILVIA IS THE WORST

Organized
and I mean **organized**
to the extreme.

She has schedules for everything
        like for cleaning (yuck)
and for eating
        or for how she washes and blow-dries her hair
every Tuesday and Friday night, no exceptions,
before pulling it back into a tight bun.

And I know now that Dad is the one
who told Janet to call her,
though why he assumed Titi would want
to babysit
is a total mystery to me,
and I wonder if he knew then
how much my aunt works
        (it's a lot)
or that I'd be spending so much time
alone here
when I could've just been
alone at Crenwood instead.

My mom and dad,
sometimes they'd be out of it for days.

So I got really good at microwaving Maruchan
and eating the free food at school,

and what I'm saying is,
I know how to take care of myself.

I'm like a woodpecker.
Or a hummingbird.
A solo bird instead of part of a flock.
Being alone is normal.
Super normal.

But the thing is,
alone is different everywhere,
and I'd rather be alone with my parents
than alone with Titi

who

hasn't even hugged me once
          and
is awkward every time she speaks
          and
has too many house rules
          and
who, honestly?

I can't imagine I'll ever love.

LETTER #1

Dear Mom and Dad,

I've never written a letter before, so this feels kind of weird. But we've also never been far away from each other and I've never lived with someone else before, so I guess the letter writing isn't the weirdest thing going on right now.

I asked Titi Silvia who asked Janet who asked her boss, and they said I could write to you. I don't really get why they won't let me call, but Titi says this will be good for my writing skills. Like I'm just magically going to catch up to everyone because I'm sending a letter every few days. She clearly doesn't know how hard sixth grade is.

Anyway, my new school gave me a computer that I get to take home, which is why these letters are printed. My teacher showed me how to say what I want to write out loud and the computer will type it for me. Cool, right? Don't tell Titi Silvia. She'd probably get mad. She thinks I'm typing these out by myself.

I looked up Harmonic Way on my computer. I hope it's as nice as the pictures and that it's a good place for you to get better. I'm doing good too. I'm still your little woodpecker, Dad! Working hard at school and making tons of new friends and following Titi's rules. So you don't have to worry about me <u>at all.</u>

Just focus on what you have to do and let me know how I can help so we can move back together really soon. I have my bag packed and am ready to go whenever!

Love from your daughter,
Laura

P.S. I'm really, really sorry.

DINNER FOR ONE

On the days Titi works at the hospital,
I'm supposed to heat up a Tupperware
and eat dinner by myself.
Today she's left me rice and beans and chicken,
but it's not as good as the kind my parents make,
and when I finish eating
I almost feel emptier
than how I was when I got home.

After dinner I take a walk
around my aunt's apartment complex,
surprised, but also not, at how completely quiet
        everything is.

And I wonder if kids even live here
if kids even play here,

which just makes me miss Crenwood
and my neighbors
and my friends.

And how over there
everything might have been a little "less"
(in Titi and Janet's opinion),
but honestly,
it was actually

a little *more*.

THINGS I'VE ALREADY DONE THAT ARE "NOT OKAY" ACCORDING TO TITI SILVIA

1. Not take off my shoes before I walk inside, which, how was I supposed to know?
2. Not leave my Rubik's Cubes lying around (the couch is not for "my stuff")
3. Not rinse dishes before putting them in the dishwasher (I've never even used one before!)
4. Not made sure to wipe any hairs out of MY bathroom tub
5. Not used a coaster for my glass of water when I'm watching TV
6. Not put the recycling in the recycling container (which is which?)
7. Not made my bed in the morning (IT'S NOT EVEN A REAL BED)
8. **Not asked for permission before going on a walk because apparently I'm "only" eleven**

THINGS TITI SILVIA HAS ALREADY DONE THAT ARE "NOT OKAY" (SHE IS NOT MY MOM)

1. Talk to me in Spanish even when I answer in English
2. Ask me about school every single day
3. Ask me questions about myself like she cares
4. Offer to blow-dry my hair
5. Check my closet to see if I've unpacked yet
6. Invite me to run errands with her
7. Buy me random things I didn't ask for
8. **Act like this isn't about to end any day now**

SPANISH VS. ENGLISH

I think if it was just the rules
or how intense she is
about wanting to be my *aunt* aunt,
I wouldn't always be so grumpy,
but it's the talking that gets to me too.
My aunt is always trying to get me
to talk Spanish,
"full Spanish,"
saying how we're
Puerto Rican
and she can't believe my mom
let me forget.

But how can you forget
something you never learned?
And more importantly,
something your parents
obviously didn't think
you needed to be taught?

Mom may have been from Puerto Rico,
same as Titi,
but she's been in the US
a really long time.

And Dad?
It's not his fault his parents
never even taught him at all.

And what's wrong with that, anyway?
I was just fine with my mostly English,
sometimes Spanglish life.
I never even thought it was a big deal
until my aunt started making it a *thing*
practically every time we talk.

You look Puerto Rican,
she loves to tell me.
Don't you wanna sound
Puerto Rican too?

And I just shrug because what else can I say?
Truth is, I don't care what I look and sound like to her.
All I care about
is what I look and sound like to my mom.

But who is gonna tell my aunt that?
Definitely not me.

'Cause I may not like it here,
and I may not like *her*,
but Janet was very clear with me—

if I don't behave, if this doesn't work out,
then I'll have to go live with a stranger
until my parents come back.

And even though I know my parents
will be all good by like the end of this week
        MAX,
I'm not gonna risk making my aunt *too* angry,
not if it means the possibility
of going somewhere even worse,
somewhere even farther,

with even more roads
keeping my family
apart.

SCHOOL UNIFORM

At my old school
you could go to school in pajama pants
and slides and a sweatshirt,
and nobody would even look twice.

Here, though?
Even though I wear the new clothes
my aunt bought for me,
I still feel like people are looking,
like my hair is a little too frizzy,
my clothes a little too uncool,
my glasses too bright and round,

and every kid in here knows
how much I'm pretending,
how much of me is a lie,

all made up,
so they won't find out the truth.

LUNCH AT THE LIBRARY AGAIN

The librarian talks to me today,
the one with the MRS. ELSA (SHE/HER) badge.
Asks if she can help me find some books
before I shrug and tell her I'm not a reader,
that books are kinda too hard.

She tells me there are no bad readers,
just books that aren't quite right,
and then she asks me if I like graphic novels,

which
just makes me sigh and frown.

'Cause it seems teachers are always trying
to give me baby books,
shorter books,
like I won't notice the characters are
second graders
who can already read better
than me.

Honestly,
the only people who've never made me
feel bad
        and not smart
about how I read are my parents,

who would skip the books altogether
and just make up stories to help me sleep.

And so I follow Mrs. Elsa,
not because I want to read her books,
but because maybe her graphic novel pictures
will at least give me ideas,

and then when I go back to Mom and Dad
I can surprise them
with the most EPIC story time we've ever had.

BIG-KID GRAPHIC NOVELS

Mrs. Elsa doesn't take me to the baby books, though—
she actually gives me stories
with girls around my age,
one called *Guts*
(a true story about a fifth grader),
and one called *The Okay Witch*,
where the middle schooler on the cover
has frizzy hair and a messy backpack,
and thick eyebrows like mine.

She tells me to let her know if I like them,
that it'll help her find me more stuff to read,
and I smile and follow her to the checkout desk,
because maybe two things can be true at the same time.

Maybe I can read *and* get inspiration for stories,
and then Mom and Dad will be happy *and* proud
and everything will be even better
than how it's supposed to be.

I AVOID BENSON IN THE HALLWAYS

I don't really know why he keeps following me,
keeps trying to be my friend,
just that every time I see him,
he makes a point of smiling real big and waving,
sticker water bottle in hand—
one time leaning over so far to do so,
he literally tripped over someone else.

And it's not that I don't want to be
friends with *him* specifically,
it's more that I don't know
how I could have any friend right now,

how I could talk to someone daily
or hang out with them,
and not have them see
how much everything in my life
is currently mixed up.

Although who knows,
for all I know, what's messed up
is not giving Benson a chance.

How do other kids ever make up their minds?
How do other kids say things
without going over it in their heads fifty times?

My dad used to say there are no bad decisions,
just bad intentions,
and that's all fine and good
but my dad isn't the one who ruined everything,
that was all me, myself, and I.

MOST OF THE TIME? I'D RATHER BE A BIRD

Like a flamingo, maybe.
Flamingos,
they make friends for life.

Which means they never have to
start over with people
never have to
explain big changes
or keep secrets,
because their flamingo friends
already know it all.

I'd be a terrible flamingo, though.
Because even though back home
I had Remedios, Betsaida, and Pilar,
even though I love them
and have known them
practically our whole lives,

and even though they know
basically everything about me,

I never told them about the drugs.
I just didn't.
Not even once.

SPLIT IN THREE

The thing none of these adults understand
is that it's not that easy to just *belong* somewhere,
not that easy to switch lives.

I'm not myself in my aunt's apartment
and I'm not myself at school,
but it's not like I can just cast a spell
and WHOOSH
turn back the clock
to be the me before everything got swirly,
to be the old
Laura Rodríguez Colón.

I wish I was older and braver,
because if I was
maybe I'd sneak out of Titi's,
find a way to get to
my mom and dad.

Or maybe what I wish
is that Titi was nicer,
would take my side over Janet's,
and just drive me to Harmonic Way.

Because how does nobody see it?
How do none of the adults understand?

If home is in Crenwood
and I'm in Stonecreek
and my parents are at rehab

how can I possibly be
the real Laura
if I'm divided
three different ways?

WORTH IT?

I feel like I've spent the last few days
tiptoeing around Titi Silvia's
hundreds of apartment rules,
but today I get home in such a sad mood
I don't even go into her place—
forget all the stuff I'm not supposed to do!

I just leave the bus stop
and go for a walk.

It's still quiet and weird,
but at least that means I can look at birds,
which I'm actually pretty good at identifying
'cause Dad is basically an expert
and he taught me well.

Not that there is a lot of variety at Stonecreek,
mostly just sparrows
hopping and chirping around.
Which makes sense since Stonecreek is
as fake a place as you can get,
with weird, perfectly trimmed round bushes
but zero trees,
like wild natural branches would be too much
for people like Titi

who I'm pretty sure would trim *me*
if she could

change me up, bit by bit,
to be less like Mom
and more like the kind of girl
who'd fit in Stonecreek better,
a Laura more like her
than me.

DID YOU KNOW?

Sparrows aren't originally from the United States,
not even from North America
or Central or South America
or any America at all.

What happened was people in New York City,
they got tired of caterpillars and moths
eating up all their trees,
and so they brought over
a bunch of birds from Europe
to eat the bugs,
not realizing how much the birds would like it here,
how much they'd want to stay.

Which is really just a perfect example
of how my dad was wrong,
and what matters isn't intentions
but decisions,

which is what I'm thinking about
as I slowly walk down the block,
when I suddenly see a dog cage
tucked under the shade of the mailbox area roof,
a big FREE DOG sign
taped to the cage,
which makes my heart start beating a little faster

because who just abandons their pet like that,
who leaves out something they love
without even trying to find it a home?

I walk over to drag the empty cage to the dumpster,
but when I walk closer
I see a big brown puppy
lying panting on its side,

and I think I gasp,
maybe yell,
'cause the dog isn't moving,
looks like it's sick
maybe dying
and I can't possibly be the only one
who has seen it around.

I back up and look in all directions,
but I'm literally the only human
in this whole stupid place,
and my heart's not just fast now
it's POUNDING
this is too much
it's too hard
too much like that morning in Crenwood

and suddenly the sun is crushing me
and there is not enough air

why am I always the one
who has to decide?!

SUPERHUMAN LAURA

I have no idea how I carry the dog
all the way back to my aunt's.
Everything is hot (the dog)
and sweaty (my hands)
and painful (my heart),
and at some point during the walk
my glasses fall off.

Somehow blurry-eyed me manages to not
run into a parked car
or trip on the stairs,
but by the time I make it to #1380 C
I am spent
and shaking
everything mixing up
in my stomach and head

and I just yell my aunt's name
all broken voice
and burning eyes
until she wakes up and opens the door.

BLURRED MEMORIES

I think my aunt tries to scold me as she takes the dog,
but I just start to cry,

and when she asks me
in a kinder voice
what happened,

all I can say in between hiccups
is

I just found them, Titi.
They weren't moving.
I was so scared I called 911.

And now they're gone
everyone is gone

and why am I even keeping my bag packed?
Why am I even trying to figure out
how to reach my mom and dad?

They're not here
and it's all my fault.

REJECTED

My aunt tells me to go do a Rubik's Cube
in my room
and she'll deal with the dog.

And I'm barely listening,
but I do register the word "room"
and somehow make my feet walk down the hall
and into the office,
where I start pacing around.

I grab my biggest Rubik's Cube,
the one that Dad got me for my last birthday,
which has five rows up and sideways instead of three.
And I sit on the floor until I've finished it,
which might have been five minutes or ten,
maybe even fifteen.

I feel dumb for crying,
because obviously this dog is nothing
like my mom and dad,

and now I probably just gave my aunt
something else to be not okay with me about,
and I wouldn't be surprised,
not even a little bit,
if this makes her call Janet
and change her mind about keeping me
after all.

SPIRALS

Laura, my aunt says,
coming into my room.

And I look up,
my brain still swirling,
waiting for her to tell me
to grab my black bag
and get in Janet's car.

But instead she says
Hay que llevar al perro al veterinario.
He needs an IV.
You know, a bag of fluids.
Porque está deshidratado.
And not really understanding, I nod.

Except she keeps standing there,
until I realize she's waiting for me to get up.
That she means we're taking him to the vet *together*
that the dog's gonna be okay after all,

that I'm not packing
I'm not leaving
and maybe I actually

made the right call.

SPLIT IN HALF

I don't remember much about what happened next—
not my aunt finding my glasses
or us driving to the vet
or the time we spent in the waiting room,
the dog stretched between my aunt's lap and mine.

All I know is we left him at the vet overnight,
and now I'm in my room
staring at the ceiling,
because Mom and Dad always said
we couldn't afford a dog.

I know what I did was right,
or at least that's what my aunt said,
but it also kinda feels like
I'm betraying my parents,
doing something they wouldn't have liked.

But the dog was so sad at the vet
tired and hurt
and left out for free
that I'd be lying if I didn't say
my heart jumped a little

because how different are we, really?

Both abandoned.
Both trying to exist.

DOG ON THE BRAIN

The days go by quickly—
or slowly—
half the time I'm not really sure
what's going on.

At school I do my best to stay invisible
to teachers and kids
(and especially Benson),
and at home I take care of the dog,
feeding him, walking him,
basically all these extra chores
I have to do now that Titi has said
the dog is actually ours.

I don't mind, though.
Even if I pretend I do.
I never realized dogs could be so soft
so cuddly—
I suddenly have a live stuffed animal
that's warm and even snores a little,
making bedtime not as lonely
as it used to be before.

But I have to keep reminding myself
that he's not really mine or ours,
he's my aunt's.

Just like this apartment
and this school
and everything she's bought me
since social services got involved.

It's confusing,
living this borrowed life.
Like I'm an actor in a movie
that could stop filming at any time.
And sure, I'm reading my lines
and following my script,
but the whole time I'm just thinking of my parents,
and wishing I could give them a call.

I've never gone this long
without talking to them,
or even without being in the same place.
We've always been a family,
the Rodríguez Colón unit,
through good times and bad times,
through thick and thin.

Except I didn't follow that.
I was the one who said it was too much.

Or at least I'm scared that's how my parents
     will see it,
because even though I know that I called
because I thought they were dying,
know that I called because they

wouldn't respond,
how do I know for sure
that that's what my dad is thinking?
Or my mom?

MY AUNT AND THIS DOG

You know when you have friends
in your classroom
who don't really get along?
They just kind of put up with each other
'cause they're stuck in the same class
but make sure to always stand
on opposite sides of the room?

That's my aunt and this dog,
even though she's the one who decided to keep him.
She's always complaining about how he smells
(*like a puppy*?)
and how he spills water every time he drinks
(um, he is *learning*)

and forget about the way she shouted
the day he ate one of her shoes.

So yeah, maybe his short brown fur does stick up
when he sees her sometimes,
his brown eyes squinting,
not in a mean way, just in an
Ugh here she comes again way.

And I'm trying really hard
to not fall in love with this dog
and his floppy ears,
'cause I'm 100 percent sure my parents will say no,
        but wow can I relate.

Because I feel like my heart growls a little at my aunt
all the time too,
and if you ask me,
Titi needs some Love 101 lessons,
'cause I'm not saying I want her all over me,
but like,
I get it, Dog,
I get it.

I wish I lived somewhere else too.

WHAT IS A NAME?

I've been trying to think of a name
'cause I feel bad that I keep calling the dog
      Dog.
But I've never had to name anything
on my own before,
always had Mom to help me with
stuffed animals and dolls,

and it makes me nervous to have to decide
such a big huge thing,
because what if the name makes Mom hate him,
or makes me love him more?

And I'm sitting on the floor with him,
tossing him his squeaky ball
and watching him jump and flop awkwardly
as he tries to catch it in the air,
when I get my lightbulb moment and tell him

I'm gonna call you Sparrow

to which he just
tilts his squishy head to the side
and drools.

But it makes sense, doesn't it?
People in the United States didn't mean to
keep the sparrows forever,

and so this name will be a reminder to myself
that like this apartment,
like this life,
Sparrow is temporary,

that unless I can magically convince my parents,
unless they come out of rehab completely new people,
Sparrow will *definitely* not be coming along.

SPARROW IS BROKEN

I never knew dogs could have
such weird personalities.
What's even weirder, though,
is how I've only had Sparrow a short time,
but I already know more about him
than I know about my aunt.

Like how his favorite thing to do
is lick me until I'm sticky wet
(gross)
and how when my aunt yells at him,
his eyes get big and sad
and he just stares at her
until she rolls her eyes
and gives him a tiny pet.

It's like he doesn't know how to dog,
the way he's scared of the slide in the park
and the mailboxes
(okay that one makes sense)
and the garbage truck
and loud birds
and even bicycles chained to racks.

Really, Sparrow is scared of everything,
which means he'd fail at protecting me
(which is what my aunt says
pit bulls are supposed to do),
but he does love to play fetch
with any ball that squeaks,
and cuddle with me at night
(even when I push him away
'cause he just gets so *hot*)
and lick peanut butter from a spoon.

Sparrow makes me wish my aunt
was as easy to figure out,
with all her rules I never know are rules
until I break them without knowing how,
things that I do my very best to remember but,
I'm not perfect, you know?

I never had to work so hard to be good
when it was just me and Dad and Mom.

MY BEDROOM: BEFORE

My bedroom at home used to be
a random mix of stuff—
a bed frame from Craigslist
Dad built me for my birthday,
a desk from Facebook Marketplace,
a lamp from the Buy Nothing group.
Decorations from Dollar Tree and
Five Below and Amazon,
and cool stuff me and Mom just found
abandoned on people's stoops.

It was cheap, yeah, but I didn't care—
just 'cause something is cheap
doesn't mean it's bad.
And my parents always made it a fun time,
a contest,
trying to find the nicest stuff
for the least amount of money,
picking stuff up at people's houses
or looking in shock at the kind of stuff
rich people threw out.

I miss it, my room.
I know Titi Silvia probably wouldn't believe me,
but I actually actually do.

And even though I've spent days
in a funk,
even though finding Sparrow
felt like slipping on ice
and falling straight on my back,

I know I can't just wait
for social services
to decide when I can get my life back,

I need to brainstorm
         need to plan
so I can move back in with my parents again
no matter what.

MY BEDROOM: NOW

Titi Silvia takes me to Ikea,
tells me to pick out
whatever bed I want,
and even though I pretend to look
at all the expensive white furniture,
I wonder why the inflatable mattress
isn't good enough,
why it always has to be shopping and new things
whenever I'm out with my aunt.

I pretend to study the nearest bed,
but then I mumble that the mattress in the office
is just fine.
Except then Titi is all:
You deserve to pick out your own stuff,
and not have to use the things for guests.
Yo sé que tú crees que no necesitas nada,
but trust me, it's time.

And I want to tell her that
I *am* a guest,
that I'm going to think of something
'cause I've already stayed too long,
but she's holding up blankets
for me to look at,
pointing out patterns and colors and shapes,

and I don't know how to tell her
that I don't want things of my own,
don't know how to tell her
that the furniture she wants to get delivered
won't make her apartment my home,

that the penguin-print comforter and purple lamp
are cute
the bulletin board and toothbrush holder
useful

but not the same as Mom and me
going on errands
and then singing in the car.

Me and my aunt?
We're not real family.
We're just an awkward adult doctor
and a kid who always messes up.

QUESTION TIME: MY AUNT

I've been thinking about this
for a while now,
and something about the silence in the car
finally makes the words come tumbling out.

Without looking at her,
eyes and hands on the Rubik's Cube
I take out of my pocket,
I ask my aunt if she would maybe drive me up
to go see my mom and dad.

Titi Silvia frowns and shakes her head,
tells me she can't do anything
without asking my caseworker first.
But then she adds that Janet is coming over
tomorrow after school, though,
so I can probably ask her then.

That Janet will visit once a month
to check in on us,
but will also be the one checking in
on my parents
to see if rehab is going well.

Would you take me, though? I ask my aunt.
If she actually said yes?
I know you and Mom always fought
and, I don't know.
You don't really seem like sisters.
Or even friends.

And Titi sighs and is quiet for a bit,
before saying,
You're right. Peleábamos mucho.
Nos mentíamos también. But Laura?
That was before. And no matter what
your mom and I went through together,

I promise

I wouldn't lie to you.

MONDAY

By the time lunch rolls around,
Ms. Holm has already taken away
two of my Rubik's Cubes,
and probably told me to focus
about two dozen times.

I can't help it, though,
'cause ever since Titi told me
Janet was coming,
all my hands and legs have done
is twitch and jiggle and tap,
until even Sarah in the desk next to me
tells me to please just stop.

I guess it's kind of hard to explain
how it feels,
not that I would try telling Ms. Holm or Sarah
even if I knew how.

It's just . . . imagine you knew nothing about anything
and then suddenly you had a day and time
to see the person
who could tell you absolutely everything,
the person who could say yes to visiting your parents—

I mean, would YOU be able to focus on math?

GUTS

The *Guts* book Mrs. Elsa gave me
is actually really good.
Doesn't feel babyish or too hard,
and I definitely get Raina
and her stomachaches,
because today I've felt sick
pretty much all day long.

But just 'cause the book is good
doesn't mean I can focus,
not enough to read, anyway,
or do more than pretend to turn pages
while I look at the clock.

And so when Benson sits down near me,
        again,
I close my book and give him a half smile,
because he really is persistent.

Even if I still don't know
why he wants to be my friend.

A little too hyper? Yes.
A little too happy? Mm-hmm.
But whenever he sees me in the hall
he asks me about my day.

And today he shows me the card trick he's working on,
and I laugh ('cause it's actually good!)
and almost forget
all the stuff in my brain.

Benson asks me about my old school
and I admit how small it was,
how Riverview's size makes me feel
tiny and invisible and a little soft,
and he nods and says he gets it,
and even though he doesn't say anything else,
I get the feeling he's being honest,

that even though he's not new,
even though he seems to have it together
and seems to have the perfect life

maybe

I'm not the only one who's lost.

QUESTION TIME: BENSON

Don't take this the wrong way,
I tell Benson,
but why are you in the library with me
when you could be outside playing ball?

And Benson seems a little unsure
about the question,
so I mentally slap myself and try to fix it,
saying:
I didn't mean it in a bad way,
just that most of the kids in my classroom
can't wait for lunchtime so they can go out.

Benson nods and plays with his braids,
not quite as excited as he was before,
and then he sighs and says:

I used to be sick.
Well, I still am sick.
I guess . . . It's not really the kind of sick
you ever get cured from.

That's why you'll always see me
with my water bottle and my hoodie, he says,
and also why sometimes I just need
quiet lunchtime to rest.

But last year I was sick more often,
and that meant canceled baseball practices
and canceled birthday invites
and days and days away from school,

and I guess the other kids,
the ones you've probably seen
rushing to get outside,
just got tired of catching me up,
of babysitting me,
of missing me,
and so they stopped
being friendly,
stopped inviting me at all.

SIXTH-GRADE HERON

I'm still thinking about what Benson told me
as the bus rolls up to my aunt's place—
how his friends just got tired of waiting,
like he was a boy only good enough
if he was 100 percent healthy and well,

and I decide then and there
that I'm not going to be
like Benson's ex-friends,
either with Benson or anyone else.

I will be patient like the blue heron,
who stands quietly in the water
until a fish splashes nearby,

and even if my parents have been taking
a little longer than I expected

(to write me a letter /
to get well)

I will still be there—
a short, frizzy-haired
eyeglasses-wearing heron,
waiting to welcome them back in.

LICKS

Sparrow is waiting for me
when I get out of the shower,
because he's silly
and likes to jump up and
try to lick the water droplets
falling from my wet hair.

I sit on the floor
to squeeze at my hair
with a small towel,
Sparrow snuggling in
as close as he can,

and even though I'm still nervous
about Janet's visit,
I smile,
because sometimes
all it takes is Sparrow
to turn it all around.

VISIT ONE: SOCIAL SERVICES

The visit is not exactly
what I thought it would be.
Instead of Janet coming in
with a ton of updates,
she asks me about school and Titi
and how everything has been.

And I try to ignore how annoyed I am,
I try to be good
and just answer her questions
and do as I'm told,
but it quickly becomes clear
that she's the kind of adult
who will never get to the point,
'cause why are we even talking
about me and my life,
when the only reason she's here,
the only reason I'm living with my aunt,

is 'cause *Janet* and the rest of social services
took my parents
and locked them up?

I finally interrupt her,
ask her when I can see them,
tell her my aunt can drive me,
that she already said yes,

but Janet sighs in that annoying adult way
and tells me that my parents
are working hard to get better
and me visiting would be
       a distraction
       a complication
that could keep them from meeting
their goals.

And I must have just stared at her,
because how am *I*
       their *daughter*
gonna keep Mom and Dad
from following their plan,
but before I can say anything,
do anything,
Janet just pats my head
and tells me to keep writing them
that that's all I can do,

and then she and Titi Silvia do that
grown-up silent eye talking thing
and send me to my room.

REHAB AND THERAPY

It annoys me that Titi and Janet
are in the living room talking without me,
because I know that means they're talking
      about me
like I'm too little to understand.

So I grab my computer
and go on the Harmonic Way website,
trying to see if Janet was lying
about visits from children not being allowed.

And as I'm clicking through their pages,
I see a picture of a golden retriever
with a bunch of happy people,
a bright red vest that says THERAPY DOG
on his shiny golden back.

And I don't know what a therapy dog is,
but my heart starts beating hard in my chest,
my eyes suddenly laser-focused
looking from the screen to Sparrow and back
because as I dictate the question to Google
I think,

forget what Janet says,
and forget my aunt,
and forget every adult who
thinks they know what's best for my parents
even though they're not my parents' kid.

Children may not be allowed in Harmonic Way
(according to Janet),
but apparently therapy dogs and their owners
are.

Which means it's time for me
to take this whole thing into my own hands.
To be the independent, strong woodpecker
I know I am.
A week, max?
And Sparrow and I will be at Harmonic Way
where we belong.

YOUTUBE: WHAT ARE THERAPY DOGS?

I watch a couple of videos,
which help me understand the difference
between therapy dogs and service dogs,
which I had definitely been
getting mixed up about.

Service dogs go through A LOT of training,
'cause they have important jobs
helping people with disabilities
and/or people who are sick,
and they definitely need to learn
how to do a lot of very hard stuff.

Therapy dogs, though,
are just regular dogs
who are very well-behaved.

And they get to visit places like schools
and hospitals and libraries and nursing homes,
basically just focusing on
making people smile and feel good
when they're having a bad day.

So yeah, I've got this.
I don't care what Big Boss Janet says.
All I have to do is teach Sparrow to be nice to strangers
and then figure out how to get to Harmonic Way
and then BOOM

I'll be with Mom and Dad
and together we can figure out what's next.

TRAINING: SIT

I've started to try to train Sparrow
'cause if I want to see my parents,
that's what I need to do.

And I don't know if he's really smart
or I'm really talented,
but even though at first
I have to push his butt down,
soon all I have to do is lift my hand
with a cookie in it
and he's plopping down all by himself,
licking his lips excitedly
for the treat he wants to chew.

We demonstrate for Titi Silvia after dinner,
and she watches us with interest,
music playing from her kitchen speaker,
hands rinsing dishes in the sink,

and then she's high-fiving me
and petting Sparrow,

and for a minute, I feel invincible,
for a moment,

I almost feel brand-new.

OTHER PEOPLE PROBABLY REGRET THINGS TOO

Even though Sparrow is learning Sit
and is pretty much potty trained,
sometimes when he gets really excited
he forgets
and pees a tiny bit on the rug.

And it's kinda stressful,
because whenever he has an accident
Titi Silvia gets so mad
I'm convinced she's gonna lose it
and send him to the shelter in town.

Puppies mess up.
That's a thing, right?
They're like babies but with fur.
And maybe that's why Titi
never had kids

because the way her left eyebrow shoots up
when he makes mistakes,
the way she rubs her head and sighs,
makes me feel like maybe
I'm not the only one
regretting some of my decisions,
maybe Titi is too.

The question is:
Who does she regret more?

Me the human? Or Sparrow the dog?

READING HELP

I've always known I wasn't the best reader.
It kinda becomes obvious
when you never pass your end-of-year
Virginia State SOL tests.

But I guess this new school cares more or something
because I haven't even been here two weeks
and I've already been assigned
extra help.

I don't mind working with Mrs. M—
she's nice and friendly
and has me practice reading with her
for twenty minutes every day.

Today, for example,
we practiced putting sounds together
(even in words that don't exist!)
and it sounds kind of silly,
but Mrs. M promised it will help.

I told Mrs. M about Sparrow,
and she actually suggested
I read to him at home.

And Sparrow is *such* a good listener
I don't even get embarrassed
when I make mistakes.

And it makes me wonder if maybe
if my parents see how Sparrow
helped me visit them,
see how Sparrow helps me read,

it might actually convince them
to let me take him home.

LAURA RODRÍGUEZ COLÓN: JUNIOR DOG TRAINER

I got a book on dog training from the school library
but it's kind of hard to read by myself.
And I don't want to ask Mrs. Elsa or Mrs. M for help,
because my aunt doesn't know my plan
and neither does Janet,
and honestly,
even though I like all my teachers,
and I used to be pretty good at trusting adults,
social services has made me paranoid,

and I don't want to risk a teacher telling Titi
and Titi telling Janet,

because I don't like Janet,

and she'd probably mess everything up.

Instead, I use my lunchtime
to look up videos on YouTube,
because YouTube is magic for kids like me.
I mean, I can learn how to teach Sparrow
anything I could ever want to teach him,
without actually having to stare
at words for hours,

without actually having to read.

BENSON JOINER: MASTER DOG TRAINER

Benson shows up while I'm watching videos—
I swear he has a sixth sense on how to find me,
always,
no matter what.

He dives onto the beanbag next to me,
loudly,
the way Benson usually is,
and he says that video is a good one,
but am I on dog training TikTok yet
because that's the place to be.

I laugh,
tell him my aunt would freak out
if I was on social media,
tell him she hasn't even given me a phone,

but then I immediately freeze up
because I just answered a question
he hadn't even asked
and what am I doing??

Was it okay to tell him just like that?

He just shrugs, though,

and takes a bite of his energy bar
(he's always sneaking them in)

and says that's cool,
that TikTok isn't all that great anyway,

makes himself comfy on the beanbag
and tells me I should ask my aunt
if we can hang out one weekend,
so he can show me what he trained
his own dog to do.

LETTER #2

Dear Mom and Dad,

I know, I know. I should wait until I get your answer before I write to you again. But what if the letter got lost, or accidentally fell out of the mail truck, and then you never get anything and I'm stuck forever waiting for you to write me back?

I have a dog now. But don't worry, I'm not trying to keep him or anything. He's temporary, and he's gonna help me come see you, so that's pretty cool. His name is Sparrow and he is a brown pit bull with a tail that wags so hard it's practically a weapon. I saved him, kind of. It was a little scary. But I think you'd be proud.

Everything else is still going great. I have a lot of friends, but my closest one is a boy named Benson. He's gonna help me train Sparrow. (Yes, this is related to the plan I just mentioned. Just wait! It's gonna be the BEST surprise.)

Love from your daughter,
Laura

MEZCLA SATURDAY

Today Titi Silvia is off from work,
and when she calls me into the kitchen,
she has a whole bag of ingredients
spread out on the marble countertop,

and I can't help wrinkling my nose
because the stuff she has out?
It does not look good *at all.*

Cans of Spam and jars of Cheez Whiz,
plus some tins of red pepper something
that look slimy and bad.

So when she starts dumping stuff
in the food processor
and tells me we're making the
sandwiches of her childhood?
Of my mom's childhood?

I sigh and sit on a stool
and wonder why we can't just make
some pb&j sandwiches
and forget this whole Puerto Rico
education thing
that I was starting to hope
she'd forgotten about.

WHY MOM DOESN'T TALK ABOUT PUERTO RICO

I guess Titi senses my attitude
(okay maybe I rolled my eyes),
'cause she asks me why I don't want to learn
when there's so much she could teach me
about the place my parents are from.

I tell her if they wanted me to learn,
they would have taught me
and it's really not a big deal
'cause at the end of the day,
we're all American
living on Virginia soil.

Titi is not convinced, though,
tappity tapping the counter with her red nails
like she wants to say more,
then sighing and saying Mom
shouldn't take out her trauma on me,
that she wants me to go to PR with her
for Christmas,
and I should learn more about the island
before I go.

And I'm all . . . trauma?
What does that even mean?

Which makes Titi sigh again,
before saying that I might as well know now,
since who knows when Mom
would have told me herself.

A tu mamá la botaron de la casa,
Titi says,
like it's no big deal for parents
to kick out their kids.
She wanted to date a girl
and your grandparents wouldn't let her,
and it turned into this huge fight
that ended with her and her girlfriend
getting on a plane
and just . . . never looking back.

MY AUNT NEVER GETS IT

'Cause I knew Mom had dated girls,
but I didn't know about her getting kicked out.
And why would my aunt ever think
that knowing THAT
would make me want to meet the people
who threw Mom out
like she was a piece of trash?

Besides, it's not like I'll still be here in December
(a whole forever month and a half away).
By then I'll be back in Crenwood with my parents,
and Puerto Rico?

It can stay across the ocean
where it's always been.

GUESS I'M NOT THE ONLY ONE WITH SECRETS

I don't see Benson at all on Monday,
not in the hallways or the library
or in the line for lunch.

And it makes me feel a little weird,
'cause I guess I didn't realize how much
I was getting used to talking to him
until I spent a day all on my own.

I ask Mrs. Elsa if she's seen him,
and she shrugs her shoulders and sighs.
Says Benson's probably in the hospital again,

like that's something totally normal,
like it's something she assumes he's already told me,

and that shouldn't worry me at all.

I TAKE MY TIME WALKING SPARROW

Mostly because my aunt is asleep
and I have nothing else to do after school
other than work on his good behavior
for the therapy dog stuff
which, despite my confidence earlier,
I'm still not 100 percent sure how to do.

But I keep thinking of Benson,
and what Mrs. Elsa said,
and how if he really doesn't have any friends,
then that means he's probably at the hospital
all by himself.

And Sparrow can tell I'm distracted.
He loves being the center of attention,
so he'll pull me everywhere if I'm not
present
        and concentrated
             and on my toes,

but even though I usually like that,
like how Sparrow makes me think just about him
and not about all the other messed-up stuff,
it's hard to focus on Sparrow and his training today
when there are so many things about Benson
I've just realized I don't know.

So even though I'm still learning the area
and the bus routes,
I formulate a plan.
Because the one thing I do know
is that the hospital Titi works at
is basically the only one around for miles,
so chances are that if Benson got sick,
that's where they would have taken him,

and honestly,
that hospital?
It's really not that far out.

SNEAKING OUT

I debate waking up Titi and asking her,
'cause she's so strict about knowing where I am
every minute of the day.
But she's always so grumpy
when she first wakes up after a long night shift,

so grumpy when I ask for permission
for things she doesn't think I should do,

that she'll probably say no,
and then I'll have woken her for nothing,
and ruined both my plans
and the afternoon with her.

So instead I kiss Sparrow's smushy head,
and then kiss it again three more times,
and even though he's usually pretty quiet,
I promise him extra treats if he doesn't bark.
Put him in the gated kitchen area,
give him a Kong toy filled with peanut butter,
and then slowly
quietly
sneak myself out.

DOMINION SPRINGS HOSPITAL

I get to the university hospital pretty quickly—
it's only a few bus stops away.
And once I'm there it's almost too easy
to say I'm looking for my aunt,
and just walk myself in.

My dad would have been really upset with me,
'cause he hates lying of any kind,

but all I can do is hope Titi doesn't find out
and snitch on me,
and that Benson is actually here
to make everything worth it,

so if I do get in trouble,
if I did make the wrong choice,
I at least made someone happy enough
to make the punishment feel
a little bit right.

ROOM #211

I find Benson fast,
'cause all the rooms in the
children's section
have the kids' names out front,

and with the kind of huge
HUGE
grin he gives me?

I don't even question my decision
like I usually would.
Don't even worry about getting grounded.

For once?
I have no doubts at all.

AWKWARD SILENCE

Once Benson gets over the fact that I'm there,
he gets pretty quiet, his face tight and eyes sad.
Says he was hoping he wouldn't have to tell me
all the details,
so that there was zero chance I'd stop talking to him
and change my mind.

I sit in the big blue recliner next to him,
and do my best to smile.
Tell him I've got secrets too,
and no pressure to share,
'cause he doesn't have to,
but he can tell me the full truth,
     if he wants to,
and I won't leave or make fun.

SICKLE CELL DISEASE

Benson tells me he has sickle cell,
which basically means his red blood cells
don't look the way they should.

That my red blood cells look like full moons,
but his are crescent-shaped
with sharp curves,
which means it's hard for them
to carry as much oxygen as mine do,
and sometimes they get stuck
and his knees and elbows hurt.

It means sometimes he gets tired,
and sometimes his joints swell up like grapefruits
and he's in a lot A LOT of pain,
and then he has to come to the hospital
for blood work and pain meds,
so that he can go back home

only to eventually
always eventually

have to come back again.

It sounds exhausting,
especially for someone who plays baseball
and has to go to school,

and my face gets all hot thinking about
his old friends
and how they dumped him,
how mean people can be,

how it seems like people are always
always
just looking for an excuse
to get rid of anyone different,
anyone who is a you
not a me.

QUESTION TIME: ME

So . . . you gonna tell me why
you live with your aunt?
Benson asks,
once he's done telling me
just how bad fifth grade was.

And I try to gulp down my shame,
'cause he was honest with me
about something really big and hard,

and the thing is,
it's scary
but I do *want* to tell him.

It's hard, pretending.
Smiling and nodding when
Ms. Holm talks about our parents
like we all live with them,

saying "mom" and "dad"
when the right word is "aunt."

It's a lot of work, and I'm tired,
and so today?

I talk.

WHO DECIDES WHAT IS SAFE?

My parents are good people, I say,
even though I have goose bumps
and it's hard to look Benson in the eyes.
I didn't get taken away 'cause they hurt me
or they're bad.
They just have a problem,
an addiction,
that sometimes makes them forget
other things in their life.

Social services was going to put me
with strangers, I tell him,
in foster care until I could go back,
but then this aunt I don't really know,
my mom's sister,
she agreed to take care of me,
just for now.

I haven't seen my parents since they went to rehab,
which is really really hard.
'cause honestly, even though my aunt is family,
she's not the kind of family that feels right.
And I don't get why Janet,
my caseworker,
gets to make that decision,
when she doesn't know anything about me and my life.

I mean, honestly?
I tell Benson,
finally looking at him,
my voice shaking a bit
from somewhere deep inside.

I don't care that they were taking pills.
I don't care that sometimes
they weren't really around.
They are my home
and all I want
every single day
is to go back to living with my dad and my mom.

BENSON LISTENS CAREFULLY

He doesn't say anything weird
or mean
or unkind.

He just says that sounds really hard
and he can't imagine starting over like that,

in a new house
with a new school
and a new family

all at the same time.

I smile at him,
glad he doesn't say anything rude
about my parents,
even though sometimes they make me
a little mad.
'Cause it's one thing for me to sometimes
wish things were different,
and another for someone like Janet
or Titi or Benson

to judge them and call them bad.

But he just listens until I'm done,
and then we keep talking about other things,
like our dogs,
and Benson shrugs and says it might sound silly,
but honestly
the worst part of being in the hospital?
Is being away from Zelda, his pug.

GOOGLE: HOW DO YOU GET SICKLE CELL?

I ask my Chromebook to tell me more that night
and I actually learn a lot of things.
The pages are hard to read,
but that's why Ms. Holm
installed that Google Chrome extension thing
on my browser,
so I can click it and have it read out loud to me
from whatever internet page I'm in.

I learn that sickle cell started in places
with a lot of malaria,
which is something you get from mosquitoes
and can make you so sick you die.
And so humans in those places evolved
to have special cells
that made them sick in other ways
like Benson is,
but protected them from malaria,
which was even worse.

One of those places was Africa,
the continent where lots of Black people were kidnapped
        from,
and so that's how we ended up with sickle cell here,
even though we don't have malaria,

'cause all those people were enslaved in the US
and then some of them passed the sickle cell genes
down to some of their kids,
and then some of *those* kids
passed it down to some of their own,
and so even though not every family passed it down,
and even though some people can have the sickle cell
    trait
without having the disease,
some kids, like Benson,
are still born with it today,

and according to the internet,

not enough people care.

BENSON VISIT #2

I don't have to worry about sneaking out today,
since my aunt is actually at work
and the apartment is empty when I get in.
And even though Titi has that Ring camera,
I'm pretty sure now that she
doesn't actually check it,
'cause she didn't say anything last night
while we were eating our bisté and arroz.

Sparrow is being so cute, though,
that I have a hard time getting up
off the floor.
One lick, I tell him,
showing him my index finger,
which he immediately licks.
Okay, also one kiss, I add,
bending over and kissing him
on his snout.
Except that just makes him go into
super-lick overdrive,
which makes me laugh,
even though Titi says dog tongues are gross.

I'm packing my backpack
when I remember what Benson said,
how what he misses most isn't school
but his dog,
and suddenly my belly starts tingling
because sure,
Sparrow isn't officially a therapy dog yet,
but like,
who even decides that?
Why not have a real practice TODAY?
I mean wouldn't going to a real hospital
be the very best way to train?

TITI SILVIA: HIKER?

I guess Titi is a hiker,
or used to be one

because in the hallway closet
I find a humongous backpack
that I'm pretty sure is made for
people leaving on long camping trips
where they have to have a bunch of clothes
and cooking supplies and
actual sleeping bags.

It's too big for me,
but it sort of fits if I adjust the straps
all the way down,
and most importantly,
and really the only reason I went looking,
is it will fit my little Sparrowy baby inside it
just fine.

THE BIG PLAN

I put Sparrow's harness on
and take him outside to poop and pee.
Then, just to be extra careful,
'cause Sparrow definitely gets the zoomies
after being alone all day,
I take him to the dog park and we play fetch
until he drops down on the grass,
too tired and happy to do anything
but follow me quietly to the bus and the bus stop,
which thanks to Janet my social worker
(and really, the only thing to ever thank her for)
I get to ride for free.

HOW MANY LETTERS IS TOO MANY?

Sparrow is quiet on the bus ride,
just napping inside the bag,
and I wonder if I should send my parents
a third letter
or actually wait for their reply.

I've never written anyone letters before,
so I don't really know how the mail works.
Like how long letters take to arrive
and come back,
or if there's a way to confirm
that they've even made it there all right.

I know I could ask my aunt,
but it's just . . .
I don't know how to explain.
Sometimes I feel like
there's this huge wall between us
and it's not even anything she's doing
it's just how serious everything seems
and how guilty I feel
even thinking about giving her a chance.

Would Mom want me and Titi Silvia to be friends?
I honestly don't know.

How can I do the right thing here
how can I decide what's right
if I don't even know what the people around me
actually want?

MY MOM TRIED TO GET CLEAN ONCE

I remember because she was extra sick for a while
but then it all started to get good.

She was awake more
the food truck open more
and we even made cinnamon rolls one morning
before going for a walk in the park
like I've seen other mothers and daughters on TV do.

The problem was Dad was still doing stuff

(in secret)

like we wouldn't find out.
And even though they ended up
having a big fight about it,
Mom eventually gave in,
started taking pills again

(not in secret),

meaning they both went back
to their regular routine,
one that didn't include me
or paying bills,

one where the food truck opened
some days and not others,

and led to the night
which led to the morning
where everything
absolutely everything
got messed up and broken

and led to me being here,
writing letters,
missing my dad's stubble
when he kissed me good morning,
and my mom's hugs
when I'd come home from school.

COMPANY

Benson is not alone
when Sparrow (in his backpack) and I
make it up to his room.

His mom (or who I assume is his mom)
is there,
but she smiles real big and says

she's glad to see Benson
making new friends, real friends,

before leaving to "go get a little pick-me-up,"
which freezes me in place before I remember
that this is Benson's mom and
not my own.

That she probably means coffee
or chips from the vending machine,
and not a stash of something
from inside her purse,
and before Benson can notice
that anything is wrong,
I force myself to smile and breathe
and say a quiet hello.

The moment she's gone
Sparrow yips,
like he can tell it's now just us in the room,
and I quickly open the bag
and let him topple out,
because forget moms and their snacks.

Benson's wide-eyed shock
turning into big belly laughs

is the best thing I've ever seen.

DID YOU KNOW?

Google says cuddling with dogs
helps people feel better.
I learned that while looking up
what therapy dogs do.

And looking at Benson and Sparrow
and how happy Benson looks
makes my own mouth arch up
into a giant grin.

'Cause I mean I know I said
I wouldn't be able to take Sparrow with me,
but
who actually knows?
Maybe my parents will be different after rehab.
Maybe they wouldn't mind me having a dog.

Benson is looking at me
laughing,
saying how this is the best day ever
because it's hard to be here in this dry,
no-dog-tongue hospital
when
he's used to a certain number of kisses from Zelda
every single day.

And for a moment I can see me and Sparrow
visiting hospitals too,
and not just Harmonic Way,
but then I shake all those thoughts right out of my head,

because this is not a forever plan,
and I need to f-o-c-u-s
need to remember
that Benson and Sparrow?

They are a tool. A path.
Everyone and everything is temporary.
The only permanent home is my mom and dad.

FOREVER FRIENDS

This is why you're my best friend,
Benson says,
which makes my body go icy and then hot,
my mind still determined to put Benson and Sparrow
in the temporary part of my brain
'cause otherwise everything
would just hurt too much.

Seriously, he continues,
I'm so glad I met you.
I'm so glad we're friends.
And before I can stop my own mouth,
I say: For now. Until I go home.

Benson immediately stops petting Sparrow,
which makes Sparrow let out a little grumpy bark,
and I can tell from Benson's face that I've said
the wrong thing,
but I don't even know how.

I'm just being honest,
I say carefully,
afraid of making things worse,
but Benson just shrugs, energy all gone,
and says:

Yeah, temporary best friends.
That's what I meant.

TROUBLE

Sparrow barks again,
almost like he's telling me I messed up,
but before I can think of something
to say to Benson,
a nurse opens the door
mouth open in shock.

And then the whole room is
exploding with noise,
and people are yelling at me
and at Sparrow,
asking about my parents,
always my parents,

as I grab Sparrow's leash
and panic-yank him
out into the hall.

And then Sparrow and I are
　　　running
　　　running
　　　running

straight into Titi Silvia's white work coat
straight into her very *very* angry
LAURA, STOP.

THE LETTER I DON'T SEND

Dear Mom and Dad,

Everything here is a mess. I don't
understand why you haven't written to me,
why you haven't come back yet, and why I'm
still living with Titi Silvia who doesn't
even care.

   Didn't you ever think this might happen?
Didn't you ever worry you'd get so sick
that I'd be all alone? 'Cause guess what? I
worried about it. I worried all the time.
And now I'm still worrying about it, except
now?

   I worry all alone.

LETTER #3

Dear Mom and Dad,

I hope you are okay. I'm sure they are keeping you so busy you don't even have time to write. On the website they make it seem like a lot of fun, but I'm guessing it's kind of like school. Fun sometimes, but mostly just a lot of work.

In school updates, I'm now getting something called reading interventions. A really nice teacher picks me up and we practice separating words into syllables. Stuff like PIL-LOW, and using different reading strategies, and honestly I think I'm getting better. I really do.

I think you would be proud of me.

I'm proud of you too. I know rehab is probably boring, but I know you are working very very hard to come back.

I'm so sorry for what I did. Please don't be mad. Write me back?

Love from your daughter,
Laura

GROUNDED

My aunt is mad at me,
so mad she can barely look me in the eye,
going on about how disappointed she is,
how embarrassed she is,
that I'd go to her job and pull a stunt like that.

Basically, now I can't go anywhere,
except to walk Sparrow for ten minutes at a time,
and she even took my laptop
and said I can't use it outside of school,
which means I can't do *anything*
except read to Sparrow and stare at the wall.

I mean, who does she even think she is?

She's *not* my mom,
she's *not* my replacement parent,
and if she thinks this is showing me she cares,
then she is even more clueless than I thought.

INSIDE EXPLORATION

I'm sitting in my room,
bored and grounded,
too blah to even practice on my Rubik's Cube,
missing my mom and our hot chocolate nights,
and my dad and our bird walk days,

when I suddenly remember the closet full of
camping stuff
and wonder if there are other treasures
hidden in there,
like maybe some bird stuff
I might use to play.

I jump out of bed
and run to check it,
because honestly,
I think there's a chance.
A lot of hikers like birds—
maybe my aunt
used to be like that.

And I can't believe I didn't check earlier,
because when I go through her stuff
I find a fancy pair of binoculars,
seriously *fancyyyyy*,
nothing like the Walmart version
me and Dad used,

and before Titi can see me
I tuck them into the elastic of my sweatpants,
yell out that I'm going to walk Sparrow
and head out to watch some birds with my dog.

BINOCULARS

In school we've studied all sorts of inventors,
Like Thomas Edison
and George Washington Carver
and Alexander Graham Bell,

but Dad and I used to google
different sorts of things together,
about birds mostly,
but also about stuff like binoculars
aka the greatest tool for any bird lover
unless maybe you own an expensive camera
that can zoom a lot.

And yeah, it's not easy to hold on to Sparrow's leash
and look through the binoculars at the same time,
but at least now I know
I can look at birds around Stonecreek,
which is something that makes me HAPPY
and doesn't require any friends
or any adults.

Just me and the birds.
And I guess Sparrow.
Who, honestly,
is probably the only one in my life
not mad at me right now.

APOLOGIES: TITI SILVIA

Titi Silvia apologizes,
which is weird,
because I don't think an adult
has ever apologized to me
before Titi sits me down.

Se me fue la mano, she tells me.
I was upset and didn't take the time
to truly see.
Didn't think about the fact
that you weren't trying to be bad,
you were only trying to help a friend.
Your only friend, maybe,
since you moved in here with me.

She says she's sorry for her reaction,
but it's important I be careful with how I act.
That she's already had to change her schedule
since I moved in,
and that she could have gotten
into a lot of trouble at work yesterday,
if her boss hadn't decided to be nice.

APOLOGIES: ME

I apologize back,
because by now I'm less angry
and I honestly didn't mean
to get her in trouble,
I just really thought
nobody would find out.

I tell her I won't do it again,
not all sneaky like that,
but that Sparrow
is going to be a therapy dog anyway,
so I honestly just thought
it was fine . . . ?
And didn't think about
how the people at the hospital might react.

I don't tell Titi *why* Sparrow is gonna be a therapy dog,
'cause I'm not sure if she'd approve
and even though I'm not sure if that's lying,
even though I'm never sure
if I should say things to her or hold them in,
I ignore the guilty swirl in my belly

because my aunt smiles at me
with that smile that almost looks like Mom's,
that smile that sometimes makes me
forget to breathe,

tells me I really am a good kid,
and that if I want to look into training Sparrow,
she'll support me,
she promises,
she'll help us be the best we can be.

GOOGLE: HOW DO YOU BECOME A THERAPY DOG?

I tell my aunt that I don't need her help.
That all I have to do is make sure Sparrow is nice.

And Titi Silvia laughs
and says nothing is ever that simple,
and if I'm actually serious,
I'm going to have to work hard.

I'm annoyed that she seems to know more than me
even though I had googled all that stuff,
but I sit on the couch with her anyway
as she pulls up some websites on her iPad
that I guess I hadn't clicked into before.

She hands me the iPad but I look at my feet,
whisper-ask her if she can read it out loud,
and even though my aunt looks at me
for a long silent moment,
she takes the iPad back
and starts reading,
and I sit a little closer,
like I used to do with Mom.

We sit like that for a while—
my aunt reading
and me listening,

Sparrow sitting on the floor
with his head on my lap,
until my aunt suddenly gets a work call
and jumps up,
and I shake myself a little
not sure how much time has just passed.

Focus, I mutter to myself.
Just focus on the training. On the plan.
Getting a dog "certified"
still doesn't seem that hard.

All the dog has to do is pass a
Canine Good Citizen Test
(pshhh—easy)
and then a Therapy Skill Test
(easy x 2),
and then they're all in
and ready to start.

WHAT SPARROW WILL BE GRADED ON ACCORDING TO THE SHEET TITI PRINTED OUT FOR ME

1. Accepting a friendly stranger
2. Sitting politely for petting
3. Appearance and grooming
4. Walking on a loose leash
5. Walking through a crowd
6. Sit, Down, and Stay
7. Coming when called
8. Reaction to another dog
9. Reaction to distraction
10. Supervised separation

WHAT SPARROW CAN DO ALREADY

- ☑ **Accepting a friendly stranger**—He's always super nice to people on our walks.
- ☐ **Sitting politely for petting**—Does this mean no licks?
- ☑ **Appearance and grooming**—I keep Sparrow's coat super shiny and clean.
- ☐ **Walking on a loose leash**—Like no pulling? Ever?
- ☑ **Walking through a crowd**—Haven't tried it but I'm pretty sure he'll be fine.
- ☑ **Sit, Down, and Stay**—He knows Sit!
- ☑ **Coming when called**—Always. Sparrow loooooves me.
- ☐ **Reaction to another dog**—Hmm. Need to find another dog. Zelda?
- ☐ **Reaction to distraction**—Good? Unless it's something that scares him (which is a lot).
- ☐ **Supervised separation**—Maybe Benson can help?

BENSON IS BACK

Except I only find out by accident,
when I see him at the cafeteria
in line to get food.
And even though he smiles
and we take our trays out to a bench together,
he just doesn't seem like himself,
all quiet and serious and in a mood.

Are you still sick?
I ask him.
And he rolls his eyes and takes a bite before saying:
I'm always sick, remember?
It doesn't go away.

No, I say,
I meant does your body still hurt?
You seem not as
      —I study him—
Excited? Hyper? I don't know.
You're missing that Benson spark.

Maybe you can't see the "spark,"
he says, his voice kind of mean,
because you're not actually my real friend.

And then before I can say anything else,
he stands up,
pulls his hood up,
dumps his food in the trash can,
and walks away.

EATING SOLO

I don't understand what is happening.
Why is Benson mad
when I've basically been the best friend I could be?
I mean I got in trouble for him,
got grounded for him,

I literally just met him and yet
he already knows
all these big big things about me,

things that my forever friends back home don't know
'cause I haven't even talked to them
since I had to leave.

Forget Benson.
I don't need the drama.
If he's gonna be a baby
then I'd rather just sit alone and eat.

TITI SILVIA: ADVICE

I'm still mad when I get back to Titi's,
which is not good
'cause my aunt is actually awake
and immediately wants to know what's going on.

Why do you even care?
I say grumpily.
Normally you wouldn't even be here
or you'd be asleep.
Like why is that okay when you do it
but if my parents do it
then all of a sudden they get locked up?

Titi Silvia goes still,
and then she tells me to come sit with her on the couch.
Sparrow comes and joins us, of course,
but she makes him get off,
'cause it's Titi,
and she only lets him get on my bed
and not on furniture in the rest of the house.

Look, she says,
I know this is hard on you,
and I know you're upset.

But I'm not a robot, okay?
And when you say stuff like that
like how I supposedly don't care,
it hurts my feelings,
'cause I'm just here
trying to do my best.

Why would that hurt your feelings?
I ask, still grumpy.
I'm just telling the truth.
But then I stop, Benson's face at the hospital
suddenly appearing clear in my brain.
Wait, I say. Is that why Benson's mad at me?
Because of what I said?

¿Qué pasó con Benson?
Titi asks,
and I tell her about calling him
my temporary friend.
And she nods and says softly:
If I were Benson,
and I liked spending time with you,
that definitely would have made me upset.

AM I A MEAN PERSON?

I'm sorry I hurt your feelings, I say,
looking down at the couch,
and Benson's too.
But I don't know how to treat people
like I'll be here always,
when I know I won't.
I know. *I know.*

I look into her eyes,
which look like Sparrow's when he's sad,
and for a second I feel something
almost like pain
but not pain,
deep in my gut,

but then Titi licks her finger,
brushes some frizz out of my face
(like I'm two!),
and I don't know why that annoys me so much,
because Mom used to do it to me
all the time too,

but I take a step back and roll my eyes,
make an excuse about homework,
and walk to my room.

VIDEO CALL

I call Benson from my Chromebook
and he doesn't answer,
so I record a voice message to leave him instead.

Say I'm sorry I hurt his feelings,
that I didn't mean to,
and that honestly,
he's a really good friend,
I just . . . I don't want to get used to life here,
because then it'll hurt more when it's over,
when my parents come and get me . . .

which I have to believe—
I have no choice but to believe—
is going to happen
very
soon.

BENSON FINDS ME IN THE MORNING

Thanks for your message,
he says,
fist-bumping me and giving me a tiny smile.
You're right. I was upset about what you said,
but I talked to my mom about it
and she says sometimes
it's good to take things slow.
That everyone has different speeds.

Yeah, I agree.
Slow is good.

But I also need your help
to be FAST about something else.

And then I show Benson the list
of things Sparrow apparently has to learn,
and his normal big smile
comes back.
Says he will help me with it,
that Zelda already passed her good citizen test
just for fun,
and that Sparrow as a therapy dog?
He'd be a rock star.
And the university hospital
is definitely always looking for more.

Benson writes down his mom's name and phone number
on a piece of paper he grabs out of his bag,
and tells me (again) to ask my aunt for permission,
'cause if both me and Sparrow can come over,
he'll be our best-friend training guide.

LETTER #4

Dear Mom and Dad,

I miss you a lot. <u>A lot</u> a lot, which you can probably tell because I'm sending you so many letters. But don't worry. I have enough supplies.

Do you like the new bird stationery? Titi got it for me. She says just because the letters are printed doesn't mean the paper can't be nice. She also got me these cute pigeon stamps, which is kind of perfect if you think about it, since pigeons are the ones who used to deliver letters way way back in time!

Anyway, it's nice being able to write to you. I like how the steps are always the same. Dictate to the computer. Print. Fold up the paper. Stuff the envelope. Seal it. Write Harmonic Way's address. Stick on the stamp. Walk to the Stonecreek mailboxes. And push it into the outgoing slot. Something just between us.

Maybe you would like it too if you tried it. Though I don't know if you have computers there. You might have to write them by hand.

I'm training Sparrow to be a therapy dog. I don't think I told you before. But that's my big plan. My friend Benson is gonna help. I wasn't being very organized about it, but now I have a list of things to do so we should be done very soon, maybe even by the time you get this letter. And then I'll be able to come see you! No matter what Janet said about rules.

Isn't that cool? Our own secret visiting plan. (DON'T TELL JANET.)

Love from your daughter,
Laura

VISIT TWO: CASA

Today a new person visits,
an older lady with white hair named Brenda
who says she's my CASA worker
like I know what that is.

When I ask her, though,
(unlike Janet)
she actually explains,
says CASA stands for

Court
      Appointed
            Special
                  Advocate
that her job is to make sure
my thoughts
and my feelings
and my needs
are actually being heard.

We talk and she asks about school,
just like Janet did,
but this time I know there's probably more coming,
so I wait in silence to see what it is.

Finally, she asks Titi if she's talked to me
about family therapy,
to which Titi sighs and says she's been busy,
like that's the only reason it hasn't happened yet.

But why do I need to go to family therapy with my aunt?
I mean, yeah, things aren't perfect,
but therapy won't change that,
what will change that
is me going back home.

I don't say that, but I do tell Brenda
it's kind of pointless to sign up for things
when I won't be around that much longer.

But she just smiles like I'm a baby and shrugs,
says nobody knows how long I'll be here
and it's better to be prepared.

That therapy never hurts,
that she goes to it too,
and she thinks I'd like it,
especially with this therapist she knows
who actually—

(and here she looks at Titi and I immediately know
she snitched)—

also has a therapy dog.

EXCUSE ME, WHAT?

I'm pretty sure I just stare at Brenda,
'cause forget the therapist and their therapy dog,
what does "nobody knows how long"
even *mean,*
but I don't like to ask questions
that I don't want to hear the answers to,
so instead I ask her
when I can call my mom.

She says she's not sure
but that at least the team will get an update on Monday,
since my parents will be calling in to the
Family Partnership Meeting,
which is sort of the first big team meeting about
"my case"
happening at the Department of Social Services
(aka DSS).

And I don't get angry often,
but it's too much,
      all this not knowing
      and Titi snitching
      and people hiding things from me
like I'm in first grade

and before I know it my skin starts to tingle
and my head starts to buzz
and my face gets bright red

and my voice sounds ice-cold when I ask:

What meeting? What Monday?
Why did nobody tell me this was going on?
Just because I'm eleven doesn't mean
I shouldn't know what is happening
in MY OWN LIFE.

Also, *thanks for telling Brenda*,
I add,
looking across the living room at my aunt.
Now I know I can officially add you
to my list of people I don't trust!

And Brenda and Titi,
they both look at each other in shock,
but Brenda immediately says she'll tell the team
I want to be there,
that she guesses I'm old enough,
that, yeah, it's my right,

that she'll find out and call me back.

And my heart's still pounding
like I ran a whole block,
even though Brenda said she'd try,

but then suddenly Sparrow is under the kitchen table,
head on my lap, eyes on mine,
and I take a deep breath and nod,
look into his brown eyes
and pet his soft warm head,

and I thank Brenda politely for listening
and say I'll wait to see
what the rest of the team says.

BRENDA-1, TITI-0

Titi says it's a bad idea,
dismisses the whole thing
practically before Brenda's mouth
can even open
to respond to my thanks.

But Brenda says she's here to be
MY advocate and not hers,
which means even if Titi doesn't like it,
even if Titi thinks it's the wrong decision,
she's not the one making it.

Which means she's not the one
who gets to decide.

SILENT NIGHT

Titi and I are both quiet at dinner,
even though she makes me
these really good fried plantains
to go with my burger,
which I know is a peace offering
'cause she hates messiness,
which means she never ever fries.

I just can't get over the fact
that she didn't tell me about the meeting,
that she didn't even want me at the meeting,
even though this isn't about her at all—
it's about MY parents and MY life.

And even though I didn't tell her
the therapy dog stuff was a secret,
I feel like she also should have known,
and I can't stop being mad about it,
being mad at Brenda about it,
even though I know it's not really
either of their faults.

Before I go to my room for the night, though,
I ask my aunt if I can go to Benson's on Saturday.
Give her the piece of paper
with his mom's info on it,

because even if we're fighting
I need to stay focused on my task.

Training Sparrow needs to be top priority now,
and nothing
and I mean nothing
is gonna hold me back.

HANGING OUT

Benson's house and family
are exactly what I pictured I'd find.
Two nice parents and a sister,
and Zelda the dog running around.

Sparrow and Zelda immediately start playing,
'cause Benson actually lives in a house
with a whole fenced yard,
and so we wait for them to get the zoomies
out of their system
before I show Benson how well Sparrow can sit now
'cause my puppy is obviously the best puppy
and learns super fast.

Benson and I review the training checklist
Sparrow needs to master,
which he says will take some time
(okay, Benson, whatever).
And then we practice a little bit of Stay,
using tiny peanut butter treats
Benson hides in his pocket,
though I don't know how much they help,
since Sparrow is definitely not as good at Stay
as he is at Sit,
and with the Zelda distraction?
Forget it. If I let him, he'd play all day.

SOCIAL TIPS

I don't tell Benson,
but this is actually the least-stressful
friend hangout
I have ever had.

No pretending,
no secrets,
just two sixth graders and their dogs,
playing around.

I do smile at him a lot,
so hopefully he gets the hint,
and maybe he does 'cause then Benson says
that for the social tasks,
the ones that Sparrow also needs to learn,
maybe his mom can drive us to the park next weekend,
and that way we can practice his behavior
with strangers
and get him extra ready to pass.

I'M GONNA MISS BENSON

I really actually am.
And honestly,
I think when I move back with my parents,
he might also miss me back.

I wonder if there's any way to help Benson.
Kinda how he's been helping me.
He said his friends are not his friends anymore,
but nothing is ever that final, right?

Nothing is ever so messed up
it can't be turned around
(I hope).

And maybe
just maybe
I could help them all make up?

FRIEND HYPOCRITE

I don't want to be the kind of person
who is secretly helping Benson get his friends back
when I haven't even talked to mine.

But it's hard to think about.
Stressful to think about.
Embarrassing to think about.
Even though I know if I wanted,
I could use my Chromebook
to give them a call.

Maybe I can ask Titi Silvia
to drive me to Crenwood one day.
Maybe the girls would understand better
if I explained everything in person,
apologized in person,

so they could look at my face
and see how sorry I am.

FAMILY PARTNERSHIP MEETING

I don't go to school on Monday,
'cause Brenda actually helped me get my way.

And the entire drive with Titi to the
social services office,
all I can think about is that I am
going to talk to my parents—
T O D A Y.

I think maybe I should be feeling something,
but my whole body feels like
it's a hundred miles away
from my head and my heart.

It's hard to explain how bad
I want to hear their voices,
but also how scared I am.
Because what if
the reason they haven't written me back

is because they're still

really
unbelievably

mad?

THE ADULTS

Janet is sitting at a big U-shaped table,
and so is Brenda my CASA worker,
and Titi Silvia,
and some people I don't know.

Like the man who introduces himself as Gary,
my guardian ad litem (what?),
and the lady named Sophie,
who says she is the mediator (again, what?),
and who places a giant speakerphone
in front of her on the table and says she'll be
the one leading today's talk.

Before I can even ask anything,
we are all writing our names and pronouns down
on these dry-erase nameplates in front of our chairs,
and Sophie the mediator is passing around
water bottles
and candy
and granola bars

like we are at the freaking *movies* or something

and telling us to quiet down
'cause we're about to start.

MY PARENTS: THE PHONE CALL

Sophie calls the rehab place,
and the phone rings
and rings
and rings.

And with every ring I squeeze my hands
tighter
and tighter
and tighter

until I can barely breathe.

When a person finally picks up,
they ask to be taken off speakerphone
to discuss,
and as every adult in the room looks at each other
and Sophie picks up the phone
and puts it to her ear,

I know something has clearly
gone terribly wrong.

UPDATES

Sophie says my parents won't be
phoning in to the meeting,
that they checked out of rehab
an hour ago.

And my body comes slamming back down to the ground
my heart about to burst right out of my chest
        because for a second
I think this means they're coming in person,
but Titi's sharp serious face
lets me know that that's not what this is.
It's not what this is at all.

Sophie starts the meeting anyway,
says the point of getting together
is deciding what to tell the judge
when we see him in court.

And that if my parents aren't going to be
completing rehab successfully,
the team will have no option
but to keep the main "return Laura home" plan
        for now
but add a concurrent plan
of staying permanently with my aunt.

I LEAVE THE ROOM

I don't care if I'm being rude
by leaving before they say
whatever they're going to say next.

Because I don't care what Sophie thinks
or Janet
or Brenda
or Gary
or Titi
or the judge,

I'm going home to my parents.
And I don't care how many other plans
the team has in store.

Brenda follows me out into the hallway,
hands me a small bottle of water
and sits down with me on the rug.
And even though I don't mean to,
even though I'm so angry
I could hit the wall,
so frustrated I want to scream,

I start crying the minute
she puts her arms around me,
the minute she gives me a hug.

BRENDA

Brenda's voice is very soft,
but also warm, like her hug.
And she does her best to explain
what concurrent means
        (at the same time)
and says concurrent plans are normal,
and just a backup,
in case my parents don't do
what they're supposed to
as the weeks eventually
turn into months.

And I hear her,
sort of,
but I also feel very far away.
Because this is not how I thought this meeting would go,
and who am I kidding?

I keep trying to pretend like
maybe it was okay I called 911,
maybe it's like when I saved Sparrow
in the afternoon heat,

but it's not, is it?

How can I trust myself
to ever make another decision,
what am I gonna do when I get older
and I'm on my own,

when the first big decision I ever made,
the whole calling 911 thing,
has turned out so horribly horribly wrong?

UPDATES, PART II

By the time Brenda and I come back in,
the meeting is almost done,
but I do hear Sophie summarizing
what was said,
and saying Titi Silvia is on board.

And I don't get it, I really don't.
Why would my aunt even want me to stay
when we don't get along?

She works so much,
and we're so different,
and honestly?

This whole "new plan" and "new goals"?
Why is that even a thing?

I'm calmer now,
can think things through,
and just because my parents checked out,
doesn't mean they didn't have a reason.
Doesn't mean they won't go back tomorrow
or the day after or

maybe they don't even need to

because they left early
'cause they got better so fast.

Doesn't the team get that this is all MY fault
and not theirs?
Don't they get that Mom and Dad *want* to get better—
they just need some help?

I believe in my parents. I do.
So why can't they?

LETTER I DON'T SEND #2

Dear Mom and Dad,

I don't know why I'm writing this letter,
'cause it's not like I have anywhere to send
it anymore. I was sad you didn't call in to
the meeting, because now they're talking about
making this apartment my permanent home. But
I don't love Titi. I promise. I don't care
about Sparrow. I only love you. Please, can't
you go back to rehab? Or if you're all better,
then can you just call social services and
tell them? I know you can do this. I know it.
Please, please don't do anything bad. I'm
sorry. I'm so so sorry. Please don't leave me.
Please.

Love from your daughter,
Laura

FAMILY THERAPY

Titi brings up therapy at dinner tonight,
says maybe she was wrong
not to want to give it a try.

And I shake my head
and eat my rice and beans,
and tell her she's not my mom,
and I don't care what Sophie said,

I'm going home.

And Titi's eyes go big and wide
probably 'cause I'm being rude,
but
that's just how loyalty works, right?
How am I supposed to be
both Mom's and Titi's Laura
without telling the truth?

My aunt doesn't make me apologize, though.
Just takes a deep breath and nods.
Says I'm right, and she's not my mom,
but that goodbye I'm talking about
may take longer than I think.

That therapy could maybe help us
talk better
and live together better,
so that we're both a little happier
with the situation we're in.

And I feel myself getting upset again,
the twist in my stomach
making me feel feverish
from head to toe,
because Titi Silvia asks me
like I actually have a choice,
like everything that has happened
since my parents got sent away
was something I decided
and not something I got told.

I tell her if she wants me to go

she'll have to make me,
and that my parents probably left rehab
'cause they missed me too much.

And then I leave the dining room table,
call Sparrow over,
go into my room,
and lock the door.

SPARROW THE BABY

I kick my backpack across the room,
then try to get Sparrow to cuddle me,
to drown out this feeling of *alone,*
but Sparrow hides in the closet and watches me
like I'm some scary monster
and not the girl who takes care of him,
the girl who gave him a home.

Oh, do you hate me now too?
I ask Sparrow in my meanest voice,
which makes him whimper
and tuck his tail between his legs.

Well, forget you,
I tell Sparrow.
You were supposed to get me in
to see my parents
and now they're gone!

So there's not even any reason
for you to be here anymore!

I stare at him,
waiting for Sparrow to do something,
say something,
but he just gives me his puppy eyes
instead.

And even though I know
I should bring Sparrow to bed
or at least say I'm sorry,
I turn my back on him,
kick my backpack again, hard,

and get under the covers of my
      too-pretty
      too-big

Ikea bed.

2 A.M.

When I wake up, the room is dark,
the only light coming from the alarm clock
Titi bought me
to help me wake up to catch the bus.

Except something is off,
wrong,
too cold,
and I realize it's 'cause Sparrow is not in my bed
like he usually is,
and everything that happened last night
suddenly comes rushing back
into my thoughts.

I turn on my bedside lamp,
the light showing Sparrow curled up
on the rug next to my bed,
and my eyes start to water immediately,
because how is it possible that
he wants to sleep near me
even after I messed up,
and treated him like I did?

Sparrow, I whisper,
and he sits up and looks at me with his
big brown puppy eyes.

Sparrow, I'm sorry, I say,
softly reaching over to pat his head.
I was upset. I didn't mean that.
And I'm sorry I scared you last night.
'Cause you don't deserve that,
you don't deserve me,
and I understand if you hate me right now
'cause it feels like I just keep doing things wrong
no matter how hard I try.

Sparrow tilts his head to the side
and wags his tail,
and I climb out of bed slowly,
dragging my blanket to the floor.

And before I know it
we're both warm inside my blanket fort
and Sparrow is licking my salty teary cheeks,

and I smile because maybe
what I said to Benson is true,
even if I only half believed it at the time.

Maybe sometimes you really can apologize
and turn things around.

YOUTUBE: DOES REHAB REALLY WORK?

I don't watch any of the videos,
'cause they're all of adults
and look boring,
and where are the videos of kids like me?

Where are the videos that will explain
why Benson can take medicine for his pain
and be totally fine,
but my parents got addicted,
couldn't stop,
even though they're big and strong?

It's hard not knowing the answers to questions,
hard having to wonder all the time,
and I wish someone would just tell me
      just be honest and tell me,
how long my parents
are actually going to be gone.

MATH HELP

On Tuesday,
Ms. Holm assigns us partners for a math project,
and I end up with Brayan,
his desk and mine pushed together
near the classroom door.

I know he likes baseball,
'cause I've seen his shirts,
so I take a wild guess and ask him
if he's on the town's youth baseball team,
and when he nods,
tell him I have a friend who used to play
and maybe Brayan knows him too.

His name is Benson,
I say,
and wait to see how he reacts.

But Brayan shifts in his seat,
his smile completely gone.
Says Benson used to be his friend
in like third and fourth grade
but
things change, he guesses,

'cause they don't really talk anymore.

SCHOOL INTERRUPTIONS

I'm trying to get some more info
out of Brayan
when Ms. Holm's classroom phone rings
and she tells me to pack up my stuff,
tells Brayan to join another group
'cause my aunt is here
and I'm going home.

I grab all my stuff, confused,
'cause Titi Silvia is supposed to be asleep,
or maybe just now getting up,
but when I walk into the office
everything I'm holding
drops
because that's not my aunt
standing in the middle of the room,

it's my mom.

SLOW MOTION: PAUSE

I yell MOM
and run into her arms,
folding myself into her big body
like I can never do with my aunt,

crying into her thick brown hair
and holding her so tight
I'd be scared of hurting her
if she wasn't holding me
just as tightly
right back.

And I keep crying *Mom* into her hair
Mom into her cheek
Mom into her neck
Mom
like I've wanted to say for hours
and days
and weeks,

my body tingling
everywhere her arms are touching me,
everywhere her love is pressing me,
my skin finally feeling *home*

but before I can say anything else—

FAST MOTION: UNPAUSE

—my mom laughs nervously,
tells the secretary I love her so much
I call her mom even though she's my aunt,
and in a second my body goes from warm
to burning
because I know, I KNOW,
that once again
I've messed things up.

I can tell Mrs. Ruby doesn't believe her,
because she immediately picks up the phone
and talks in a low serious voice.
And just as my mom
starts pulling me toward the front doors,
the principal shows up.

Ma'am, I'm gonna have to ask you to leave,
he says quietly,
or I'll have to call the police.

And my mom starts backing up toward the exit
but her hand is still holding mine real tight,
and even though our school doors
aren't locked from the inside,
I can already see several other teachers
blocking anyone from getting in or out.

Mom, what are you doing, I whisper,
sweating because I know what she wants me to do,
but I don't know if that's right.

I want to go with her,
I want to go with her so bad,
but I don't want us in trouble,
I don't want *her* in trouble

and what about Sparrow
and Titi and Benson and school

and everything around us is
getting louder
faster,

and I can tell Mom sees the fear in my eyes,
I can tell Mom sees that I'm not brave enough
to make a decision like that,

and so instead of answering,
she kisses my hair
     once
     twice
and then she's gone,

and I'm standing in the middle of the office
without her,

tears falling down my cheeks,
surrounded by people
but once again
forever again

alone.

SLOW MOTION: PAUSE

I think someone makes me sit.
I know someone calls my aunt.

But time seems to stretch so long
I can count the minutes in between my breaths,
the days between each tear
the months it took for Mom's fingers
to let go of mine

and all I can think is

Why didn't I go?

TITI IS VERY UPSET

I know because she immediately
came to get me,
but hasn't spoken a word to me since.

We're halfway to the apartment
before she finally talks,
and even then she opens and closes
her mouth a bunch of times before
she finally starts.

Laura,
¿tú entiendes lo que acaba de pasar?
she asks me.
Do you get why the school was scared
and angry and about to call the cops?

I decide to ignore the questions,
too tired and heart-hurt to do anything
but press my forehead against the window glass,
but she continues and says
if my mom had taken me
that would have been kidnapping,
and she could have ended up in jail.

And that's when I feel something
rip in my chest,
because HOW
how can my own mother kidnap me
when I've literally lived with her
my whole entire life?

You don't care about me, I say,
and I feel the truth burning my mouth.
You and social services just want to
make yourselves look good
want to punish my parents for something
that's not even their fault.

You never loved my mom
and you've never loved me,
and you don't even care
what happens to me
AT ALL.

RUNNING

I wait until my aunt is showering
before quickly dumping out
my school backpack
and packing it back up.

Some clothes
some water
some snacks
my aunt's binoculars
and a Ziploc bag full of dog food
to get us through the night.

I know running away
doesn't make sense, okay?
I know my aunt will find me,
or Janet will find me

      someone will find me

but I just need at least a few hours
to think about things
all by myself.

And so I take Sparrow and leave the apartment,
sprint down the stairs,
then take off toward the back of Stonecreek,
where I know there are some trails
that eventually lead to a pond.

I've never gone there before,
'cause I know my aunt wouldn't like it,
but today I'm mad enough not to care.

And so I run,
Sparrow next to me,
the sky pink and purple from the end of the day,

run

until it's hard to breathe
until we get to the pond
until I can hear the geese,

and then I sit on a bench
and put my head in my arms
and ask myself
yet again

why I didn't go with Mom.

DID YOU KNOW?

Geese basically have the perfect
bird families.
The parents mate and then stay together
their whole entire lives.
And even after their babies
grow into adults,
many hang out with their parents,
travel and feed together,
for a very long time.

I don't know where we got it wrong.
People.
Or at least my people.
Or no,
maybe just me.

Maybe if I had called my aunt
instead of 911,
she would have helped us,
would have helped my parents
without social services getting involved.

But how would I have called her?
I didn't even know who she was.
And I don't know whether to be angry at her for that,
or angry at my mom.

All I know is by now she's probably noticed I'm gone,
'cause she's always watching me like that,
and I don't know why I care whether she's worried,
why I care whether my mom is worried,
why I care where my dad is,

because right now?
None of them are here.
It's only me and Sparrow.
Just like it always is.

HEY, SPARROW

I don't know how long we stay by the pond.
Long enough that it gets dark
and the lampposts turn on,
long enough that Sparrow curls up to nap at my feet,
and I start wishing I had brought a hoodie,
because the night is actually kind of chilly
and I left mine at home.

I bite my lip at that thought,
realizing I called Titi's apartment *home,*
but before I can think too hard on it
I hear some twigs snap
some leaves move
and then a soft
      Hey, Sparrow
      Hey, Laura
as my aunt comes up to the bench
and I scoot over to make some room.

Sorry, I whisper,
'cause I know coming here
was not the best thing to do.
But my aunt just sits down next to me,
pets Sparrow,
and says she knows I was upset,
that today should not have happened at all,

but that I was smart to bring Sparrow
because he loves me
and will always protect me
no matter what I do.

I sneak a sideways look at her
and see her eyes are puffy and red
like mine probably are too,
and then she sighs and says:

Yo sí te quiero, Laura.
And I was really scared
when I realized you were gone.
I do want your mom to get better.
She's my sister!
Her living a good healthy life
is honestly all I want.
But right now,
she's not my priority, you are,
because you also deserve to be taken care of, to be safe,
and I know I can do that for you.

I don't say anything for a while,
just swing my legs back and forth under the bench.
Because I get what my aunt is saying,
and I am
weirdly relieved?
that she is sitting here with me,

but now that I've hugged my mother?
Lost her without saying goodbye

all
      over
            again?

What exactly am I supposed to do?

SICK DAY

I pretend to cough the next morning
so Titi Silvia will let me stay home.
And maybe it's the conversation
we had last night, by the pond,
because even though I'm pretty sure
she knows I'm faking,
she still says okay
and gets ready to leave for work.

Remember I have a camera on the door,
she shouts back as she grabs her keys off the hook,
but also call me if ANYTHING
seems off, or you see something weird
while walking Sparrow,
anything weird at all.

I know she means to call her
if I see Mom and Dad,
but I honestly don't *want* to see them anymore,

because now that a whole night has passed
I keep thinking about what Titi said before
about jail.

And I know I've made a whole lot
of bad decisions already,
but I'm definitely not gonna be the reason
my parents get sent somewhere worse than rehab,
nope, no sir, no way.

Plus, if I'm being honest
I'm also kind of mad.
Because yeah, like Titi said,
none of this is fair,
but how hard is it to just stay at rehab,
get healthy

and THEN come back?

TRAINING: STAY AND COME

It seems pointless to practice things with Sparrow
now that I know my parents are gone.
But part of me thinks maybe they'll go back to rehab,
and honestly,
I need something to do
with someone who won't talk
or make me cry,
and right now that's Sparrow
weird as that is
to realize.

We mostly work on Stay and Come
with little chunks of biscuit treats,
and when Benson Zooms me
in the afternoon,
I feel like I might burst with gratefulness

for a dog that will forgive me
and a friend who knows the truth,

because I guess if I can't be at Crenwood

and I absolutely had to pick,
this is the backup option
I'd probably choose.

GOSSIP TRAVELS FAST

Benson already knows
and he's not even in my class,
which means probably all of
sixth grade does,
which means tomorrow
is gonna be *a blast.*

Benson listens to me anyway, though,
which honestly really makes me
feel good,
because lately it seems like
all the adults in my life listen, sure—
but just so they can tell me what to think
or what to do.

Do you think people can change?
I ask Benson,
thinking mostly about my mom and dad,
but also about Brayan
and all of Benson's other ex-friends.

And he tugs on a braid and shrugs
and says he doesn't know,
that he hopes so,
but sometimes it's really hard to tell.

Would you try again? With your friends?
I ask him,
and he's quiet for a while
before shaking his head.

I'm scared, he admits,
and it feels nice to hear that.
Because I want my mom and dad to get better,
and I want to believe in them,
but just like Benson,
I'm scared.

LETTER #5

Dear Mom and Dad,

I'm mailing this to Harmonic Way in case
you go back there. I hope you do.

I've been thinking about you a lot.
Janet says the only way I can go back to
you is if you get clean and do what they
say. And yeah, I hate that social services
is in charge, but wouldn't that be nice? Us
all together? No fights. No money problems.
Lots of food. No getting sick?

You can do it. I know you can. Maybe
you even already have. Is that why Mom came
to get me? Just call Janet and explain,
please. She says you have her number.

I just want you back.

      Love from your daughter,
      Laura

DID YOU KNOW?

Scientists have studied African gray parrots,
because they're one of the smartest birds
and famous for being able to work in teams
to make decisions
on how best to act or what they should do.

In the experiment,
scientists gave them puzzles
that the parrots had to solve with a friend,
and each time
the birds were able to team up
and complete the team task
in order to get the reward.

But given a choice
between partner work and solo,
some birds chose solo,
even if the team task had a bigger reward,

and I didn't used to understand that,
because why would you ever
choose less food over more,

but now I kind of get it.

Because maybe my parents
are those parrots,
not doing what people expect.

And maybe I just need to trust them.
Trust that they know what they're doing.

Trust that when it matters,
they'll want me with them.

That the alone won't last forever
and then we'll be a team again.

GOODBYE, OR SEE YOU LATER?

Titi spends a lot of time at work
and I spend a lot of time at home.
I mean, I have Sparrow,
and we work on his Stay and his Come,
but other than Benson,
I don't really talk to anybody else,
not even Brayan,
even though Ms. Holm
continues to partner us up.

In the beginning I'm paranoid,
thinking I see my mom
outside school,
or my dad at the entrance
to the Stonecreek dog park.

It's like I'm stuck on a roller coaster
of my own imagination—
I see them and my heart soars,
I see them and my heart drops,

because I don't know if
I actually want them to be there or not.

The more the days pass, though,
the more Titi shakes her head
when I ask her if they've shown up
at the rehab place or Janet's office at DSS.

And it hurts. It does.
Like maybe my mom was asking me something
when she came to my school,
was giving me a second chance
to take back that 911 day
and make it up to her and Dad.

And I guess I chose the wrong thing
because now I think maybe,
when my mom left me at school,

she wasn't planning on coming back.

TWO STEPS FORWARD, ONE STEP BACK

There's a lot of things I've learned
since living with Titi.
Like how to load the dishwasher
and how to vacuum,

or how it's actually kinda

     nice
     cozy?

to always know where my aunt is
and to have dinner at the same time
every single night.

But this week it feels like
everything I was starting to like
before my mom came
now feels like pajamas
that are way too scratchy and tight.

Because who am I turning into?

I'm not the same Laura
I was with my parents,
but I don't know if that makes me angry
or just sad.

The worst part is, though,
that now when I hug Sparrow
all I want

is to never have to say goodbye.

AFTER-SCHOOL

We've finished packing up for the day
when Ms. Holm's phone rings,
which means I'm in the middle of a really good part
in *Saving Chupie*,
a new graphic novel Mrs. Elsa lent me yesterday
after I gave her *Manu* back.

And Ms. Holm winks at me
('cause she knows the class phone
makes me a little jumpy now),
and then she nods, hangs up,
and tells me this afternoon
I won't be taking the bus.

She says my aunt came to pick me up today,
and to just head to the office—
even though there's a whole ten minutes left
till the dismissal bell.

And so I go,
and my aunt takes my backpack and walks me out
before saying
          We're going to see that family therapist today,
like we'd actually discussed it before.

And it's weird.
Part of me is annoyed,
'cause I'm tired of doing things
just 'cause the team wants me to,
and this seems like something people do
when they're going to be together a long time,

but also?

My aunt is carrying my backpack for me
and she lets me pick the music
when we get in the car,
and I guess it wouldn't be the end of the world
if we got a little bit better
at having family talks.

READYCHILDREN THERAPY

We walk into a building
painted a bright fire-truck red,
and I can't help but smile
when I see that the lobby
is full of Legos and books
and dolls and even a train set.

Like it's not a building full of therapists,
but a playroom,
a place for kids to feel comfortable
and not sad.

Way way better
than the social services office,
so honestly,
at least there's that.

And when the doctor comes out
with just some normal-people clothes on,
I think maybe
maybe
everything will be all right.

ME AND DR. T

The doctor's name badge says
DR. TASH (THEY/THEM)
and they have me come in alone,
say it's better if we start off individually
and then merge into a group,
that way they know the kinds of things
me and Titi Silvia want to be working on.

And yeah, Dr. Tash's office is nice,
but the best part is Brenda was right,
and Dr. T has a dog,
a sleepy-looking cream Labrador
lying on a plush gray bed near the door.

Dr. Tash says that's Ivan, and he's very very nice,
so I sit down on the floor next to him,
and pet him
while Dr. T asks me
what's been going on.

For a moment I consider being difficult
but I'm honestly so tired
I don't even care anymore,

and so I tell them about Titi Silvia
and my parents
and how everything was supposed to be short-term
but now the whole team is acting like
this is my forever life.

I tell them I do believe that my aunt cares about me
but I'm scared she doesn't actually want me,
no matter what she says.
Otherwise, why wouldn't she have visited me
before this, before everything,
and tried to be my aunt
instead of my mom?

QUESTIONS WITHOUT ANSWERS

Let's focus on that,
Dr. T says and I shrug.
Has your aunt ever said that to you?
That she doesn't want you around?

And I think they're trying to say
it might all be in my head,
which I've already wondered
(like that day at the pond)
but it's just so hard to know
what Titi Silvia is feeling
what I even want her to be feeling,
so I say nothing instead.

Laura?
Dr. Tash asks softly,
but I look at Ivan instead of them.

No, she's never said that,
I admit.
But then why did she only show up
after my parents had left?

And why does she work so much
and have so many rules,

and go on and on about Puerto Rico
and who I "really" am?

And

(I feel my throat close up)

if she *does* want me
then why doesn't she ever hug me
like my mom and dad?

Have you told her you want hugs?
Dr. T asks
and I shrug.

Who asks for hugs?
Adults should know how to give them.
No questions asked.

DOG PARK

Why don't you ever hug me?
I ask Titi the next morning
as she drives me to the dog park
to meet up with Benson and his mom.

And Titi's cheeks turn pink
as she mumbles that she's not a hugger
before awkwardly dropping me off.

I try to shake off her answer
because I feel weird for bringing it up—
instead I practice walking Sparrow up to random people
and greeting them,
and also walking Sparrow over to say hi
to dogs he's never met.

It's funny how friendly people are
in dog parks,
'cause I'm pretty sure nobody says hi like that
when they're walking around town,
but something about dogs makes people braver,
something about Sparrow makes ME braver,
because I don't even worry about whether
I'm wrong or right.

Sparrow's doing so well I even practice
leaving him with Benson and walking away,
but Sparrow lets out the kind of howl
that I feel deep in my belly,
the kind of howl I want to sometimes
let out myself,

and I think maybe this is a skill
we both need some practice with,

this watching people say goodbye
and believing in them enough
to calmly stay.

CONFESSIONS

I don't know why I'm still doing this,
I tell Benson.
All the training and the checklists and stuff.

What if my parents don't go back to rehab?
Then who cares if Sparrow passes the test or not?

Benson scooches closer and takes a sip of water.
I care, Laura.
You and Sparrow visiting me at the hospital
was the best part of those boring days.

And, yeah, I don't know what's gonna happen
with your parents,
but if you like training Sparrow,
if it makes you happy just for you,
then go for it,
'cause you're gonna make
a lot of other people happy,
you're making *me* happy,

and that's worth something too.

BENCH TALK

After training practice, we let Sparrow and Zelda
run around in the off-leash park,
and Benson and I sit at one of the picnic tables,
so he can sit in the shade and cool off.

You know, I tell him, adjusting my glasses,
Janet and them think my life is so much better now.
I mean they don't say it, but they think it,
and I get that it might look that way,
you know, from the outside in.

I have more stuff now
and a "better" school
and there are no pills in my house
and Titi never skips work
and I don't ever have to make my own food.

But it really wasn't bad with my parents
and I don't understand why DSS
doesn't see that, doesn't see how
I love them and they love me,
how much it hurts,
like actually physically hurts,
to live without them here with me.

I make little designs in the dirt with my sneakers,
nervous like I always am when I talk about home,
but Benson nods and says
that just 'cause social services is in charge
doesn't mean they know everything

and my chest gets all warm when I tell him:

Benson?
I didn't mean what I said before.
You know we'll always be friends, right?
No matter where we're living
no matter what place we call home.

EX-FRIENDS

One minute we're talking
and I'm feeling good,
the next Benson freezes up
like he's seen a ghost.

I follow his eyes, suddenly jumpy,
even though I know there's no way
my parents are at the park.

But all I see is a kid our age,
Brayan, actually,
now that I look more closely,
pushing a stroller
and laughing with his mom.

That's Brayan, Benson says,
'cause he doesn't know
that I already know.

He was one of my friends.
On the town baseball team,
Benson continues.
You know, before everyone
just disappeared on me
and started leaving me out.

And I think about how sad Brayan looked
when I asked him about Benson in class.
And how sad Benson is
when he talks about the past,
and I poke him and whisper:

Maybe you should talk to him.
Maybe he feels bad too
but doesn't know how to go back.
Like how I keep not calling my old friends
not because I don't want to,
but because I'm scared it's too late,
that too much time has passed.

Benson doesn't look convinced
so I continue:
I mean, we were just talking about this
the other day, right?
How people can sometimes (maybe) change?

And Benson looks at me and bites his lip,
and I'm sure he's gonna say no,
but then he nods to himself and stands up.
Yells out
                    Brayan!
and waves him over,
even though I can practically
hear his heartbeat thumping through his shirt.

And even though Brayan looks confused
shocked
uncomfortable,
like he doesn't even know how to react,

he says something to his mom
and starts walking over
and I breathe deeply 'cause finally

I'm repaying everything Benson has done for me.
Finally, I'm helping Benson out.

AWKWARD

Listen, it doesn't go smoothly,
because how could it?
But it also doesn't seem to go all bad.

I say hi to Brayan,
and ask him something about our project,
and then I pretend to go check on Sparrow,
while sneakily peeking back.

And hey, both boys might
have their hands in their pockets,
but they're talking,
actually talking,

and I even think I see Benson smile.

And in that moment I promise myself,
no matter what,
that when I get back to my aunt's
I'm gonna get on the Chromebook
and I'm gonna message my friends.

It's been too long.
Enough is enough.

FAMILY THERAPY SESSION #1

This time it's all three of us in the room,
and when Dr. T asks me if I want to tell
my aunt what we talked about last time,
I tell them I'd prefer if they did,
so Dr. Tash recaps as I sit on the floor
and pretend to be focused on Ivan
and not Titi Silvia's face.

My aunt seems surprised about the whole
how can you love me when you were never there for me
    thing,
and then she turns and says,

Laura, you wouldn't know this,
but I actually asked your mom
to let you stay with me when you were a toddler,
después del accidente tan feo aquel,
and then again when you were in first grade.
But both times your parents said no
and then seemed to be in recovery and . . .
No sé.
Pensé que quizás todo estaba mejor.

I'm shocked,
and at first I think she's lying,
because even though Dad's told me
about the car accident,

told me that's how the pills started
and how it wasn't their fault,
I don't remember my aunt ever calling,
ever being in my life,
and I especially can't remember things
being "so bad" that my aunt would feel the need
to all of a sudden volunteer to be my mom.

I sit with that,
not sure how to feel about my aunt
trying to get me to live with her
in the before,
but then my eyes fill with tears
because if she really did try when I was little,
then why did she stop?

If she had tried harder,
I could have called her
instead of 911.

Obviously she didn't care *that* much.

She probably wanted my parents to fail
wanted them to get sick,
wanted an excuse to come in like a superhero
instead of someone who was actually our family

loving us all along.

REAL TALK

So what you're saying,
I finally answer back,
voice shaky and slow,
is that you're not actually
on Team Rodríguez Colón at all.
You knew what could happen
and you still disappeared,
still left me alone,
and you want my parents to stay sick,
because you probably think
you can do a better parenting job.

Eso NO fue lo que yo dije, Titi Silvia says.
I've told you this before.
I want you to be able to be with your mom and dad.
Your mom is my SISTER, Laura.
I love her more than you could ever know.

I don't answer her, just grab a mini Rubik's Cube
from the basket on Dr. T's table
and wait to see what else my aunt will say.
Except what she does is stand up from her chair
and sit on the floor beside me
and whisper:

Laura,
you're right. I never should have stopped trying.
But that doesn't mean I'm not Team Rodríguez Colón.
It's just that right now,
in this moment,
I'm kind of Team Laura above everything else.

And I don't say anything,
because I can feel my eyes burning,
and hate how much of a crybaby
I've been these past few weeks.
But it seems like I don't just keep making
bad decisions, I also
keep making bad judgments,
hurting my aunt's feelings
over and over again,
like I'm some sort of grumpy molting bird
so focused on my own stuff,
I can't think about anyone else.

Because Titi Silvia's eyes are soft,
and she's slowly stroking my hair,
and she's telling the truth, I think,
which makes my chest ache
as I immediately feel bad for what I said.

But before I can think about
how I always get things wrong,
Dr. Tash says they're proud of us,
and that we've worked really hard on talking
and maybe all of us could use a little break.

And so for the rest of the session we all just
color together,
sharing colored pencils and markers,
and these cool coloring sheets Dr. T says
are made for when people are worried or stressed,
and before me and Titi leave
I ask them for some extra pages,
'cause maybe me and Titi can color together sometime
like Mom and I used to do when I was younger
and she was sick in bed.

I mean, yeah.
Everything is different now,
sure,
but maybe some things can also stay the same?

RESERVOIRS ARE FULL OF BIRDS

My aunt wakes me up the next morning,
and by the time I yawn and put my glasses on,
she's already tossed two life jackets at me,
      one kid-sized,
        and one for a dog.

I barely understand what's happening,
but my aunt says it's a surprise,
and when we all walk out of the apartment
(even Sparrow)
I see her car with a kayak mounted on top.

Titi Silvia says she used to do this with my mom,
which makes me smile,
and by the time we get to the reservoir

(which apparently is a lake
that the government uses
to give us water for our pipes)

I'm wide awake and so is Sparrow,
who runs up and down the dock
barking his happiness out.

The water here has
bunches and bunches of wigeons
aka fancy Virginia ducks,
and I point them out to Titi,
the turtles too,
although the turtles scare Sparrow when we paddle past,
and I'm glad we're all wearing life jackets
'cause we almost end up in the water
before he calms down.

Laura, have you thought about Puerto Rico?
my aunt says after we're far from the turtles
and just paddling quietly around.
If you really don't want to, we won't go,
but I know everyone really wants to meet you back home.

Christmas can be such a hard time . . .

I feel her take a deep breath behind me
even though I can't see her face.
And, well, she continues,
I don't know what will happen with your mom and dad.

But if you're still with me, if we're together,
I'd really like to bring you with me to the island,
and I've looked into it,
and the thing is, we could bring Sparrow as well.

I stop paddling,
letting my aunt guide us along the still waters
as I watch some geese sunbathing on a rock.
Do they still hate my mom? I ask quietly,
and I feel Titi set her paddle down
and let the kayak drift.

No, they don't hate her, she says.
They're really sorry.
They made a mistake,
a big one,
and have been apologizing to her ever since.

Your mom, she can be stubborn,
and I'm not saying she's wrong,
she's definitely not wrong,
but they want to have a relationship with her
and I hope one day
maybe she'll want that too.

And I don't know if I'm ready
to meet all these people my mom left,
people she didn't want me to meet before,

but she's also not here,
and neither is Dad,

and instead I'm with Titi
who Mom didn't want me to meet either,

and I guess nothing is as black and white as it used to be

when I lived with Mom.

THINGS ARE BETTER

Titi Silvia and I aren't magically best friends now,
but I guess our conversations
and therapy
have helped us both share more things
in actual words.

I confess to her that I took her binoculars,
and she says I can keep them,
which makes it seem
like some of the heaviness has been lifted, sort of,
even more layers of that ice wall melted
  by this gift
  by our chats
by the way #1380 C is starting to feel normal and not bad.

How long can you be away from somewhere
before your memory starts to fade?
How long do you have to live in a place
before it becomes your home?

How many dogs and people
and unpacked bags
does it take to make a family,
and can I have
  more than one family
without giving anything up?

Dear Mom and Dad,

Titi and I started family therapy. It's
okay. Dr. T is really nice and they're
helping us be better about talking to each
other. It's weird, talking to Titi. I guess
a lot of things I was thinking about her
weren't true. She also told me you guys
were sick before. So sick she got worried
and tried to take me home with her. But she
also said you got better, which means I
know you can do it again.

I hope you're somewhere safe. I hope
you're together. I hope you go back to
rehab and I can visit you with Sparrow so
we can be a family again soon.

I think you'd like Sparrow. Titi says
she thinks you'll let me keep him. I used
to think there was no way that would happen
but I'm learning that maybe I need to trust
her a little more.

I'm going to trust you too. There are
probably some things we should talk about
together. But for now, I just hope this
letter can reach you. You always know where
to write me back.

Love from your daughter,
Laura

P.S. I'm going to give this letter
to Brenda. Titi says Brenda can mail
it if she finds out where you are,
even if that's not at Harmonic Way. I
guess what I'm trying to say is . . .
don't hide from me. I haven't
forgotten you. Please don't forget me.

SUPERVISED SEPARATION

Titi Silvia takes me to the park,
because I want to practice having Sparrow stay
even when there are lots of distractions around.

It's the hardest thing for him,
and the hardest thing for me,
but it's the only thing still standing
between Sparrow and an A-plus.

I make myself take a deep deep breath,
and then signal to my aunt,
who smiles and says:

Hi, would you like me to watch your dog?

And then I nod and give her the leash,
and walk all the way out of the park and to the car,
far enough away that Sparrow can't see me
or hear me,
and I crouch and count the seconds,
waiting but not hearing
a single sad howl.

And when enough time has gone by,
I walk back toward my aunt,

see Sparrow sitting quietly,
though his tail starts wagging
the second he sees me come back,

and I can't help it,
I jump in the air and yell

YES, WE DID IT!

and then my aunt and Sparrow are jumping with me,
and my aunt and I are hugging tightly

and I almost
almost feel
like woodpecker Laura has turned into a big strong eagle
flying happy and free.

GOOD CITIZEN TEST

Testing day comes up before I know it,
and I'm basically a bundle of nerves.
Sure, Sparrow can do all the things
but what if he really likes the tester
and wants to lick up their whole face?

What if the place is full of scary sounds
or scary things
or even worse, what if *I'm* the one
who messes up?

Honestly, I probably would have backed out
if Titi Silvia hadn't agreed to pick Benson up too,
because wow does it help
to have my best friend in the car with me,
someone who will make me laugh,
and make Sparrow happy
and not care if Sparrow's hair
gets all over his clothes and shoes.

I can tell my aunt is excited
because she keeps saying how proud she is
of both me and Sparrow,
so much so that she even let Sparrow give her one
(only one)
short lick on her hand,

and I'm not gonna lie,
it feels really good to hear her say that,
feels really good to see her do that,

because maybe
I'm starting to sort of love my aunt.

10/10

Sparrow passes the test,
and I honestly have no idea how.
I had to take so many deep breaths,
had to shake so many nerves off,
I don't know how Sparrow was able to focus
was able to perform
when I felt like I was barely hanging on.

It helped, though,
to have my aunt and Benson cheering,
to have messages from my Crenwood friends
on the Chromebook—
it helped a lot to have people who care.

And I don't know where Sparrow and I will go
with all these skills,
assuming he passes his next test,
but maybe it's okay to figure it out as I go.

Because my parents DO need help
and maybe I didn't actually mess up.

Maybe I did what I thought was best.

And maybe Dad was right about intentions,
right about wanting to do good.

And maybe that applies not just to me
but to my aunt,
because if Titi Silvia can believe in me,
really truly believe in me,
maybe I can believe in her too.

Dear Laura,

I'm sorry we never answered all the other letters you sent us before. Rehab is hard, and I was angry, and your dad was feeling sick, and it was hard to focus on the things we should have been focusing on, which is you, our forever love.

We are back at Harmonic Way, which I guess you can tell from the address on the envelope. Your dad and I . . . well, we still have to figure some stuff out. But we are on the right path for us, even if it's a different path than yours right now. And we both want you to know that none of this is your fault. I am glad your aunt is taking such good care of you. We used to have an apartment together and she used to take really good care of me too.

I love you, Laura. And so does your dad. We love you so so much. And I want you to keep sending us letters, because they will remind us when things get hard of the good things to come. Either way, I think I'm going to start trying to be a little more like you. Forgiving. Hopeful. I will always be grateful that your dad and I raised someone with such a good heart.

Janet says if we stay clean, the judge will probably allow us visitation after the holidays. That means you and I can hang out, and it's the first step toward living together again. It's probably going to be a slow process and I know this is a lot for us to say and to promise. But we're trying, Laura. We really are.

I am so proud of you. Thank you for believing in me.

Love you forever,
Mom

DID YOU KNOW?

In some bird flocks,
adult birds help take care of all the babies,
not just their own.
And I used to think that was a little weird,
because why would an animal
help another animal just because?

But things are different now.
I'm not the same Laura.

And yeah, Titi Silvia is still not my mom.

But you know what?
Sometimes things happen
that are really hard.
And sometimes that means we have to shape

homes
and nests

in other places
and with other people in our flock.

So today? Right now?
I'm okay with living in Stonecreek.
I'm okay with Titi Silvia's love.

I love my aunt.
And I love my parents.

And eventually
eventually
we'll all make it
to where we belong.

AUTHOR'S NOTE

Dear Reader,

Although this book is a work of fiction, it shows one of the many ways a family can exist. Not every kid lives with their parents. Many live, either temporarily or permanently, with other relatives or guardians.

If this was your first time reading about foster care or kinship care, I hope you better understand some of the reasons kids might live with an adult other than a parent. I hope that you rooted for Laura and her whole family, and I hope that when you meet classmates in similar situations, you are able to act like Benson and be an accepting, kind friend. And if you saw yourself in Laura, I hope she helps you figure out what home means to you and how you can hold space for family that is both close and far away. Situations like these are not always easy, and they're not always fair, but I hope this book brings you comfort in some small way.

I also hope you, like Laura, learned something new about the magic of therapy dogs. I've been able to work with many over the years and have seen how much joy they can spread. If you have a dog you think might be a good fit, I encourage you to talk to an adult in your life about getting your pet trained. (Please don't sneak the dog into a hospital, like Laura did!) We need more dynamic kid-dog duos bringing tail wags and love to those who might be having a tough time.

Thank you for reading, friend. Laura, Sparrow, and I are so happy to share this story with you.

Love,
Andrea

ACKNOWLEDGMENTS

Not only is this book about a dog, but it was also written next to my two sleeping pups. It seems fitting, then, to start the shout-outs there. To Indi José, my grumpy man-baby, who will be almost thirteen by the time this book comes out, and to my Sparrow-inspiring Ghosty (middle name also José, even though my husband insists it's not): I love you both with all my heart and can't believe how fortunate I am to work with the two of you by my side.

A huge thank-you again to my agent, Rebecca Eskildsen. I am so glad to still have you championing my work—I'm so lucky, and I know it! I can't imagine a better advocate. And to Tricia Lin, my editor once again, who continues to excellently balance making me feel great with telling me the things I need to improve, ha ha. I hope we get to work on more books together in the future. Your editing is absolutely wonderful.

To everyone else at Random House Children's who embraced this book with just as much love as my first. Katrina Damkoehler, for yet again designing a cover I am absolutely in love with, and to Oriol Vidal, for a cover illustration that melts my heart every time I look at it. Thank you also to Ken Crossland, Barbara Bakowski, Rebecca Vitkus, Caite Arocho, Catherine O'Mara, Kelly McGauley, Natalie Capogrossi, Erica Stone, and Kris Kam.

Thank you to my husband (who was just my fiancé back when I wrote *Iveliz Explains It All!*), for making sure he did everything he could to help me transition to writing full-time, and who added me to his insurance so I could still go to therapy. Supportive partners like that are kinda rare—I'm so happy we said yes together.

To my best friends—Kris, Tashay, and Amanda—for yet again keeping my mental health as stable as possible through writing sprints, book clubs, game nights, and more. What would I ever do without our (*checks phone*) over half a dozen active group chats?

And speaking of chats, a shout-out to my Bookstagram community. Y'all are still my favorite space on the internet, and I am so grateful to have internet friends to talk about books (and life!) with. Thank you especially to Samantha Augustine, my fellow Bookstagrammer and authenticity reader, for helping me get Benson just right.

Thank you, of course, to J & A, the girlies I parented for a few years. Even though Laura's story is nothing like theirs, they're the ones who first opened my eyes to the different ways family shows up for each other. I love you both and am so proud of everything you've accomplished.

Finally, to my family, but especially to my mom. She came up with the idea for an early chapter book series about therapy dogs over a decade ago, and I'm so happy to have finally been able to bring the heart of it to life. In my book, Laura is an avid bird-watcher, and that's because my mom is as well. Thank you for always supporting me.